The Misadventures of
Seldovia Sam

WRITTEN BY
Susan Woodward Springer

ILLUSTRATED BY
Amy Meissner

ALASKA
NORTHWEST
BOOKS®

The Misadventures of Seldovia Sam
This edition © 2018

Originally published as
Seldovia Sam and the Very Large Clam
Text © 2003 by Susan Woodward Springer
Illustrations © 2003 by Amy Meissner
Seldovia Sam and the Sea Otter Rescue
Text © 2003 by Susan Woodward Springer
Illustrations © 2003 by Amy Meissner
Seldovia Sam and the Wildfire Escape
Text © 2005 by Susan Woodward Springer
Illustrations © 2005 by Amy Meissner
Seldovia Sam and the Blueberry Bear
Text © 2005 by Susan Woodward Springer
Illustrations © 2005 by Amy Meissner

Editor: Michelle McCann
Original book and cover design: Andrea L. Boven / Boven Design Studio, Inc.

Alaska Northwest Books®
An imprint of

GRAPHIC ARTS
BOOKS®
GraphicArtsBooks.com

GRAPHIC ARTS BOOKS
Publishing Director: Jennifer Newens
Marketing Manager: Angela Zbornik
Editor: Olivia Ngai
Design & Production: Rachel Lopez Metzger

2018 LSI

Library of Congress Cataloging-in-Publication Data is on file

ISBN 9781513261669

Proudly distributed by Ingram Publisher Services

Printed in the U.S.A.

Contents

Bering
Sea

Arctic Circle

Yukon River

Kuskokwim River

Susitna River

Denali △

Anchorage

Homer

SELDOVIA

Kodiak

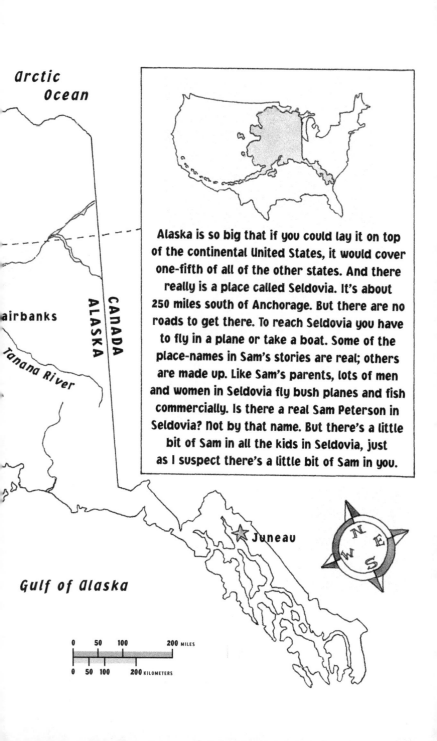

arctic
Ocean

ALASKA
CANADA

airbanks

Tanana River

Alaska is so big that if you could lay it on top
of the continental United States, it would cover
one-fifth of all of the other states. And there
really is a place called Seldovia. It's about
250 miles south of Anchorage. But there are no
roads to get there. To reach Seldovia you have
to fly in a plane or take a boat. Some of the
place-names in Sam's stories are real; others
are made up. Like Sam's parents, lots of men
and women in Seldovia fly bush planes and fish
commercially. Is there a real Sam Peterson in
Seldovia? Not by that name. But there's a little
bit of Sam in all the kids in Seldovia, just
as I suspect there's a little bit of Sam in you.

Juneau

N
W   E
S

Gulf of alaska

0   50   100   200 MILES

0   50 100   200 KILOMETERS

Seldovia
Sam
and the
Very Large Clam

Contents

1

The Too-Big Boots

Deep within his quilt and his scratchy-warm wool blankets, Sam turned over. He heard early morning sounds rising from the kitchen below. There was a soft, low whistle, then the skittering of dog toenails on linoleum, and finally the door opening and closing.

It was Dad letting Sam's dog, Neptune, outside for her morning routine. Then Sam heard the *wh-h-r-r-r* of the coffee grinder and the clanking of pans on the big gas range.

Dad's footsteps fell on the stairs, and his deep voice called, "Sam. Time to get up."

Sam burrowed farther under the covers and pulled the pillow over his head. It muffled the sound of his father's voice.

"Come on, Sam. The clams won't wait."

Sam was excited to go clamming with his father, but it was awfully hard to leave his warm bed.

Wh-o-o-os-s-h-h!!! Off flew the covers! Sam drew his legs up like a scared hermit crab as the cold air hit them. He opened his eyes, blinking.

Dad stood over him, smiling. "I know it's tough to get up, Sam, but we have to get moving or else we'll miss the good clam tide."

Dad handed Sam his clothes and Sam shivered as he hurried into them. He followed Dad down the narrow wooden steps and hopped across the cold floor on his bare feet. He scrambled up onto a stool next to Dad.

"Good morning, love," said Sam's mother.

She placed a steaming bowl of oatmeal in front of him, and planted a kiss on top of his rumpled head.

"'Morning, Mom," replied Sam, as he dove into the oatmeal.

"I wish I could go clamming with you two, but I've got early flights today," said Mom. Sam's mother was a bush pilot. She flew a small plane that carried people and supplies back and forth from Seldovia to the bigger towns across Kachemak Bay.

Outside the kitchen window, the sky was still dark. Sam could barely make out Neptune, waiting patiently on the porch. He washed down his oatmeal with a big glass of juice.

"I brought your new boots inside to warm up a bit," said Dad. "You'll want to throw on an extra pair of socks."

Sam stared at the shiny black rubber knee boots. *Ugh*, he thought. Sam grabbed two thick pairs of socks out of the dryer and

pulled them on his feet. He frowned as he slid his foot into one of the stiff boots. Even with two socks on, he could move his foot all around inside.

"Mom, these boots are so big," Sam complained. "I wish I could have a pair of hip waders like Dad."

"Sam, we went over this yesterday," said Dad patiently. "Hip waders are too expensive for a kid who's still growing. These knee boots are the smallest ones Mr. Murphy could find for you at the store."

"As fast as you're growing, those boots will be a perfect fit by next week!" teased Mom.

Sam smiled halfheartedly. He loved Seldovia, but sometimes not being able to drive to the big stores to buy exactly what you wanted was a real pain.

How in the world would he be able to walk through the gooey clam mud in these clown-sized boots?

2

Trip to the Clam Beach

T ime to load up, Sam. Grab your stuff and let's hit the road."

Dad pulled his wool coat from a peg on the wall, as Sam yanked a warm sweater over his head and shrugged into his canvas jacket. He lumbered out the door in the big rubber boots. Sam and Dad loaded the pickup truck: buckets, a sturdy shovel, a short-toothed rake, and a digging spade for Sam.

"Okay, Neptune," said Sam, "Up you go."

Neptune leapt into the truck and Dad closed the tailgate. Mom juggled an armful of stuff and set aside her radio headset and big black flight logbook.

She handed them a thermos of coffee, one of cocoa, and a sack full of peanut butter cookies.

"Save these for later, when you're done digging clams. The wind is supposed to blow hard this afternoon so I suspect we'll quit flying early today. I should be home in time to help with lunch."

"Thanks," replied Dad as he kissed her and slid behind the wheel. "Be careful up there."

The truck pulled out onto the dirt road. As soon as they were out of sight of their house, Sam and Dad looked at each other, grinned, and without a word, opened the sack of cookies.

Carefully, Sam unscrewed the thermos lids and poured steaming cups of coffee and cocoa. He knew to fill the cups only halfway. One of his first jobs on Dad's fishing boat was to fetch coffee from the galley stove for

Dad and the crew. If a wave hit the boat a certain way, a full cup of hot coffee could spill and cause the men to say words that Dad thought a boy Sam's age shouldn't hear.

The truck passed the Seldovia airstrip

with its rows of bush planes. Sam could hear an engine warming for the day's first flight across Kachemak Bay. Soon Mom would be there in her little blue-and-white Cessna, taking off from the dirt airstrip and soaring high over the sparkling water to Homer.

As Dad and Sam headed toward the clam beds at Jakolof Bay, the road dipped down into Dark Creek Canyon. The floor of the sunless canyon seemed like the bottom of the world. When the truck started up the other side of the canyon, the engine strained and sputtered. Dad had to set his coffee mug on the dashboard and downshift. The truck lurched and the empty buckets in the back fell over and rolled, crashing into the tailgate. Sam looked at Neptune. She stood nose into the wind, black ears flying. The noise didn't bother her. In fact, she looked as though she might even be smiling.

The road wound back up along the cliffs high above Kachemak Bay. On the left, the land dropped away and Sam could see the ocean far below. Dad slowed down so Sam could look at his favorite eagle's nest. Sam craned his neck to look for signs of life in the nest, but the eagles must have left already for a beach somewhere, feeding on an early spring run of salmon.

In the distance, a string of islands stood just offshore. Sam always recited their names for his father.

"Ready, Dad?" asked Sam.

"You bet, Sam. Go for it."

Sam took a deep breath and called out, "Herring-Hesketh-Yukon-Cohen-Sixty-Foot Rock!"

"Right you are, Sam," said Dad.

The road descended for several miles, and then, through the forest, Sam glimpsed the water of Jakolof Bay. The weathered boat dock came into view and Dad slowed down. A man working in a big wooden skiff straightened up and waved. It was Dad's fisherman friend, Gil Chambers. Up popped another head, a smaller one.

Oh, no, thought Sam. *It's Melody Chambers, the know-it-all queen of Seldovia Elementary School.* If Dad stopped to talk, Sam would be trapped! He'd have to be nice to Melody. YUCK!

3

Digging for Clams

Just as Sam had feared, his father brought the truck to a stop.

"Howdy, Wally. Taking the boy out clamming?" Gil called. Uh-oh, Melody was headed their way.

"Yep," answered Dad.

"I don't know why you even bother," chirped Melody, leaning against the truck window. "Those clams in Jakolof Bay are so puny. The ones on MacDonald Spit are much bigger. That's where I always go."

What a pain! thought Sam. Melody believed she was smarter than everybody, and she was always full of advice. Sam couldn't stand it.

"That's what you think . . ." he started, but his Dad elbowed him. Hard. "Uh, thanks for the tip, Melody. We'll have to try it there sometime," Sam finished.

Sam was disgusted as they pulled away from the dock. He resolved to find the biggest clam ever. That would teach Melody.

Dad pulled off the road and carefully eased the truck onto a dirt track. The truck tilted crazily as the tires climbed over some huge spruce roots. Then, suddenly, the track spilled them out of the woods and onto the beach. Sam loved the crunching sound as the tires rolled over empty clam and mussel shells.

The tide was very low. The exposed beach stretched almost halfway across Jakolof Bay. Rising from the beach were three little humps, each supporting a few spruce trees. At high tide the water would surround the humps until they became islands, but for now they were completely dry.

Dad let down the tailgate and Neptune sailed out. She wagged her tail, barked, and danced in excited circles. Dad handed a bucket and spade to Sam, shouldered the rake and shovel, and started walking.

Sam's new boots left huge prints in the sand. He put his bucket over his head, stretched his arms in front of him, and pretended he was a terrible, big-footed, bucket-headed monster.

Before long Dad and Neptune were far ahead. Sam tried to run to catch up, but in the big rubber boots his feet seemed to stumble over every single stone. Thankfully Dad stopped and Sam caught up.

"Well, this spot looks as likely as any," he decided. "Let's get to it!"

Dad began to dig. It looked like hard work to Sam. Soon Dad was pulling small white clams the size of little cookies from the mud at the edges of the hole. Sam helped, squatting on his heels and picking out clams. In a nearby pool of water, Sam swished the mud from the clams and put them carefully in the bottom of the bucket, so as not to crack their shells. They seemed awfully little to Sam, but he knew they would be just right for chowder. He worked quietly alongside Dad until the big bucket was almost full.

I would like, thought Sam, *to find a very large clam.*

He looked up and down the beach. His gaze fell on the farthest dry island.

"I'm going to try digging by that island," Sam announced to his dad. *Surely I can find a very large clam way out there,* he thought to himself. *No one digs there, and I bet the clams grow huge.*

Dad laid down his shovel and looked at his watch.

"You'd best be quick about it, Sam," said Dad. "In fifteen minutes the tide will be turning to come in. Do you see that big rock there, the one with the driftwood log next to it?"

Sam nodded.

"Don't go past that rock, and make sure you keep an eye on the water. Okay?"

"Sure thing, Dad," replied Sam, as he tossed his digging spade in his bucket and scampered off down the beach. Neptune ran along beside him.

The receding tide had left pools of water, and Sam and Neptune splashed through just about all of them. A tiny ripple in one pool caught Sam's eye: it was a wriggling eel! The slippery eel was impossible to catch as it slid through Sam's fingers.

Just wait until I get my hands on a very large clam, thought Sam. *I won't let him get away.*

Sam turned over a rock in another pool

and peeled off an orange starfish. Thousands of clear tube-legs waved gently in the air. He looked for a giant clam in the mud under the rock, but all he saw was a baby crab. He picked it up carefully and held it out to Neptune.

"Careful, girl—it's just a baby, but I'll bet it could still pinch your nose," Sam warned the sniffing dog. "Don't worry. Clams don't have pinchers."

Sam wandered from pool to pool, finding squishy nudibranchs, spiny sea urchins, and brittle sea stars. But no large clam.

Under every rock and strand of kelp was a new and glistening treasure. Sam passed the big rock and the driftwood log without even noticing them.

When would he find that clam?

Just as he was about to give up, Sam saw something near the last island. It was a huge stream of water shooting up from the mud like a geyser.

"Look, Neptune!" cried Sam, jumping up and down with excitement. "Could that be the squirt of a very large clam?"

4

Wrestling the Monster Clam

Sam grabbed his digging spade and raced to the spot. As he stepped on the soft mud next to the clam hole, another geyser shot up. *Whooosh!*

"Yeee-ha!!" hollered Sam. "This must be the king of all clams!"

Sam dug quickly. Neptune stood on her hind legs and snapped at the flying mud. The tip of Sam's spade struck something hard.

Could it be?

But it was only a rock. Sam pried the rock out and kept digging. He hit another rock, and another, and another. Sam's arms were getting tired. As he dug, cold seawater

seeped into the hole, making it even harder.

Would he never find this monster clam?

Finally, Sam's spade scraped something . . . it felt like the edge of . . .

. . . another rock? More water gurgled into the hole and the soft muddy sides started to cave in. Sam scooped out the icy water as fast as he could. He wouldn't give up now. He was too close.

He found the hard object again. It was the edge of . . . *dig, dig, dig* . . . the shell of . . . *dig, dig, dig* . . . *oh, my goodness* . . . **A VERY LARGE CLAM!**

Sam threw down his spade and began digging out sand with his hands. He knew that the shell would break if he were careless and hit it too hard with the spade. Breaking the shell of a clam would kill it, and Sam knew that dead clams are not safe to eat. Besides, how could he show off a broken shell to Melody Chambers?

He sat back on his heels to rest a moment.

Sweat was pouring off him now. Even with the shell still partly buried, Sam could tell that this was the biggest clam he had ever seen. Neptune whined in his ear.

"Settle down, girl. We've almost got him."

Finally he was able to get his hands around the clam and pull. It didn't budge. The suction of the mud was too strong.

Neptune whined again and nudged Sam's arm with her nose. Sam pushed her away.

He gently worked the tip of his digging spade under the clam and pried up carefully. He scraped a little and pried a little. He scraped and pried a bit more, and then . . .

Sshhl-l-u-c-k! The clam popped loose with a big smacking noise. Sam lost his balance and fell down suddenly—*kerplop*—into the wet kelp. There, cradled in his hands like a muddy jewel was . . .

A VERY LARGE CLAM!

It was bigger than his hand.

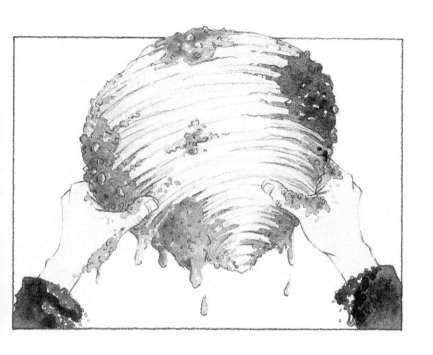

It was bigger than both his hands cupped together.

It was even bigger than the foot of Sam's boot!

Sam stood up triumphantly and said, "Come on, girl. We'd better get going. The tide will be coming in soon . . ."

But Neptune was gone.

As Sam turned toward shore, he saw

his bucket float by. The big rock and the driftwood log were gone, covered by fast-rising water. The water was now between him and the shore.

Oh no! thought Sam, *I'm trapped!*

5

Stranded!

Sam took a few steps toward shore. His boot sank in the soft muck and wouldn't budge. Bone-freezing water poured over the top and ran down inside, soaking his sock! Sam yanked his leg as hard as he could. Out popped his bare foot, his sock left behind in the stuck boot.

Just as Sam was about to panic, he heard Neptune. She was standing on the third hump, which was now an island completely surrounded by water, and she was barking at him frantically!

"There you are, girl!" Sam said with relief as he wallowed toward the island. Barnacles

and broken shells stabbed at his bare foot, but he was too scared to stop. Finally, he fell exhausted onto the beach next to his dog.

He caught his breath and glanced around. To his great dismay, he realized they were stranded!

Sam looked across the rushing water to the shore. He saw the tiny figure of his father, bent over his clam hole. Sam cupped his hands around his mouth and yelled,

"H-e-l-p . . . Da-a-d . . . He-e-l-p!"

Nothing.

He might as well have whispered. The wind and the roar of the incoming tide drowned out his voice. Sam tried again, yelling until the last squeak of air had left his lungs.

"H-E-L-P . . . DA-A-D . . . HE-E-L-P!"

Far away, his father stood up and looked in Sam's direction. Sam jumped up and down, waving his arms wildly. His poor foot landed on more sharp things, but Sam barely noticed. Dad gestured and waved back. Sam stopped jumping and listened hard.

"Sta-a-y put, Sam. I'll go get he-e-l-p!"

Sam picked up his digging spade and his clam and climbed higher onto the little island. The water was still rising all around him. He sat down in the long yellow grass. His bare foot was icy cold and was bleeding where the broken shells and the barnacles had sliced the skin.

Neptune flopped at his side and put her head on his knee. Sam watched the tiny figure of his dad hurriedly gather up the clamming gear and run for his pickup. The truck, so small it looked like a toy, raced up the beach and disappeared into the woods.

Sam stood and turned in a slow circle. It seemed like just minutes ago that the whole bay was one big beach. Now there was water everywhere! The current swirled as the tide rushed in, carrying a mess of brown seaweed and smooth driftwood.

Sam wondered how high the water would rise.

Would it cover the top of the little island before Dad could bring help?

6

Sam's Rescue

Sam felt his insides squeeze in panic. Then he remembered how to read the high-tide line. Dad taught him once when they were fishing in the bay.

Sam stretched out on his stomach and leaned over the edge of the island. He peered down at the ledge below, and there, halfway up, was a scummy green line. Below that line, the rocks were dark with algae from the sea water. Above the line, the rocks were pale gray.

Sam was pretty sure he would be safe here even at the highest tide. At least he hoped so. He sat back down in the grass, hugging his knees to his chest, and shivered. He had gotten pretty wet digging up that clam and his bare foot was aching from the cold. He shivered again, and pulled Neptune close. Overhead an eagle hung in the sky. As it flew beneath the weak spring sun, its shadow washed over Sam. It made him feel even colder, and very alone.

Sam's stomach growled . . . loudly. Neptune pricked her ears and cocked her head at him. *What I wouldn't give for one of those peanut butter cookies,* thought Sam.

Then a new worry began to gnaw at him.

He had disobeyed his father!

He went beyond the big rock and didn't pay attention to the tide. Worse, he lost a brand new boot, not to mention a bucket!

I'll bet Dad is furious, thought Sam. *I'll probably be grounded . . . forever!*

Then new worries crept into Sam's head. Maybe Dad drove too fast and the truck ran

off the road! Maybe he couldn't find a boat at the dock! Sam was getting hungrier and colder by the minute.

Neptune bolted up and stared intently past Sam. Straining, Sam could hear the faint drone of an engine. He jumped up, but his

sore foot made him sit right back down.

"Hooray! Here comes Dad!" cried Sam.

He watched and listened, but the noise flew overhead. It belonged to a little plane. Maybe it was Mom, and she didn't even know he was stranded down here. Tears welled in Sam's eyes, and he rubbed them away with his fist.

"I will never, ever disobey Dad again," vowed Sam, " . . . if only . . . if only . . ."

Then, the whine of another engine caught his ear. Slowly, it grew louder and louder as Sam stared harder and harder out at Jakolof Bay. Then, there it was! In the distance, a skiff was heading toward the little island. As it got closer, he could make out two figures.

One of them was Dad!

The engine changed to a lower pitch and the boat slowed. Dad's face was a mixture of anger, worry, and relief, but he threw Sam a grin.

"Someone here call for a taxi?" called out Gil Chambers, who was driving the boat.

Sam was so happy he wanted to cry.

Gil brought the boat around to the sloping side of the island as Neptune barked and wriggled in greeting. Dad hooked one leg over the side of the boat, hopped out, and waded onto the beach. His strong arms swooped down and gathered up Sam. Neptune leaped into the boat, skidding across the wooden seat. Gil shifted into reverse and backed the boat away from the island.

Dad rumpled Sam's hair and kissed the top of his head. Sometimes Sam felt like kisses were for little kids, but not today. He nestled against Dad's chest. He was glad they hadn't brought Melody.

"Sam, what happened to your boot?" asked Dad.

Oh yeah, thought Sam, his happiness ebbing away. *The boot.*

"It got stuck in the mud and the water came in and I couldn't move and I pulled as hard as I could and my foot flew out and the boot stayed stuck," explained Sam, all in one breath.

Dad was puzzled. "What in the world were you doing way out there? I told you not to go past the big rock."

Sam hung his head and stared at the floor of the skiff.

"I saw this big clam squirt and so I ran to dig it up. You wouldn't believe it, Dad. It's huge . . ."

Suddenly Sam realized that he had forgotten the clam and his spade back on the island!

Oh, no! thought Sam. *All that digging and freezing to death for nothing!*

7

Rescue of the Clam

The awful look on Sam's face told Dad everything. The two men exchanged glances. Gil winked at Sam, turned the skiff around in a tight arc, and headed back toward the little island.

"Thanks, Gil. We owe you one," Dad said with a sigh. He seemed about as tired as Sam.

Gil cut the engine and tilted up the outboard motor to clear submerged rocks as they drifted up to the island's beach again. Dad jumped out and pulled the bow of the boat onto the sand.

"Stay here, Sam. I'll find them," he said.

From the skiff, Sam directed his father

to the yellow grass at the top of the island. Dad quickly found the digging spade and the prized clam. He returned to the boat and pushed off. Gil started the engine with a single sharp pull of the cord.

Dad held up the muddy clam and stared at it, as if it were the clam's fault all this had

happened. Then he lowered the clam over the side of the boat and into the water.

Was Dad going to drop the clam back into the bay? Was that going to be Sam's punishment?

When Dad's hand came back up with the big white clam still in it, Sam realized he was just rinsing it off. Phew! Sam tried not to crack a smile. He knew he was still in big trouble.

Dad pulled a wool mitten from his coat pocket and carefully slipped it over Sam's foot. It felt scratchy, but warm.

Gil nosed the skiff up to the Jakolof dock and Dad climbed out to tie the bowline. Gil cut the engine and tied up the stern. Melody stood on the dock with her arms folded, looking down at Sam. He couldn't meet her eyes. He just KNEW she'd make some smarty-pants remark.

"Thanks again, Gil," said Dad, "I'm glad you were here."

Gil grinned, "I was ready for a break anyhow, Wally. Happy to help."

Gil paused from lighting his pipe. "Sam, do you think I could take one more look at that giant clam of yours?"

"Sure," said Sam. He looked at Dad, who reached into the pocket of his coat. Out came the clam. Even in Dad's big hand, it still looked huge.

"Wow!" exclaimed Melody. "That's the biggest clam I've ever seen!"

Sam smiled to himself. She must have forgotten her claim that ALL the clams in Jakolof Bay were puny!

Dad reached his big hand into the skiff and pulled Sam onto the dock. Then he crouched down.

"Climb up on my back, Sam," he advised. "You shouldn't walk on that foot."

"So long, Gil," Sam called as they headed up the dock. "And thanks . . . for everything."

Gil lifted a hand in salute. Dad opened the door of the truck and deposited Sam on the seat. The truck was warm from sitting in the sun, and suddenly Sam felt very sleepy.

8

Grime and Punishment

Sam slept all the way back to Seldovia. He slept as they passed the islands and MacDonald Spit. He slept as they passed the eagle's nest and Dark Creek Canyon. He even slept as they passed the airstrip, now busy with planes taking off and landing.

Then something shook him awake.

"Come on, Sam. Climb aboard. We're home."

Sleepily, he wrapped his arms around his father's neck as he was carried into the house.

At the sight of his mother frowning in the

kitchen, Sam finally woke up.

She'd ground him for sure!

But Mom didn't say much. She dragged a
dining room chair in for him to sit on and
fussed over his foot. Dad brought in an old
washtub that Mom filled with warm water

and Epsom salts.

"Put that foot in here, Sam, and don't you move it an inch. Do you understand?"

Sam nodded solemnly. He stared at the water as the grime and sand melted off his foot.

"I'm going outside to help your father unload the truck."

Great, thought Sam. *They're going to figure out some horrible punishment for me.*

Sam stared into the washtub. His foot stung and throbbed all at the same time. He hadn't realized how sharp those clam-shells and barnacles could be.

The kitchen door opened and Mom and Dad came in with the bucket of clams.

Uh-oh, here it comes, thought Sam.

"Your father and I have decided . . ."

Now, I'm really in for it.

" . . . that your sore foot should slow you down long enough to think about your disobedience," said Mom. "And you had a good enough scare being stranded on that island, so we're not going to ground you."

That's it? wondered Sam. *I can't believe it!*

"However," Dad continued.

Uh-oh, the dreaded "however."

"If you're going to work with me on the boat someday, you're going to have to learn to respect the tide and the sea. The tide doesn't slow down just because you're having too much fun playing in the mud. You're also going to have to learn to listen and follow instructions. I can't have a deckhand who doesn't pay attention."

Sam nodded miserably. He dreamed of deckhanding for Dad when he was older. He was mad at himself for acting like a little kid. Still, this was pretty light punishment.

Maybe if he looked really sorry and pathetic, he could get off with just the lecture.

Not so lucky.

Time to Eat!

Mom looked stern as she said, "Sam, for the next six weeks, you'll be forfeiting your allowance to help pay for a new pair of boots."

"Yes, Mom," mumbled Sam.

There went his spending money for an upcoming class trip to Homer. *Oh well,* he thought, *it could be worse.*

"I've got to rinse down the tools and check on the boat," Dad said to Mom. "If you'll make lunch for us hungry clam-hunters, I'll fix a chowder for dinner."

"Sounds good," replied Mom, "as long as you throw in your buttermilk biscuits."

"It's a deal," smiled Dad.

Sam watched Mom work. She steamed the giant clam in a little water until the shell opened and the clam inside was firm. Then she cleaned dark green algae out of its stomach and chopped the clam into pieces.

"Sam, this really is the biggest clam I've ever seen," said Mom. "Imagine—one clam feeding three people for lunch!"

She dipped each piece in beaten egg and then rolled it in bread crumbs and cornmeal. In a heavy cast-iron skillet, Mom heated bacon grease until it sputtered. Then she tossed in the pieces of breaded clam and fried them until they were golden brown.

Dad stamped his feet on the mat and came through the kitchen door: "Smells great in here!"

He sat down and Mom gave them each a small heap of fried clam. Sam's very large clam was absolutely delicious—hot, buttery, and salty fresh like the sea.

After lunch, Dad rubbed stinky ointment into the sole of Sam's foot and wrapped it in a clean, soft piece of old sheet. Sam helped him shuck all the little clams for the chowder they would have for dinner.

Dad set a big pot on the back of the range and brought a little water to a fierce boil. He placed handfuls of clams in the pot until their shells steamed open wide. Then, he removed them with a big slotted spoon into a bowl to cool.

Using a small knife, Sam scooped the clams out of their shells and into another bowl.

Next, Sam helped his mother chop potatoes, onions, carrots, and celery. Dad strained some of the cooking water from the clams into a bowl, then rinsed out the big pot and set it back on the range. Dad cut up a slab of bacon and browned it in the pot with some garlic and the onion and celery. Then, he added the potatoes and carrots and

the cooking water from the clams.

When the potatoes were soft, he dumped in Sam's bowl of shucked clams. Dad grabbed a can of creamed corn from the pantry and added it to the pot. Mom chopped fresh

parsley, and shook in rosemary and dill.
Then on went the lid, and down went the
heat.

Last but not least, Dad stirred in rich
canned milk. Together with his homemade

biscuits, this was the tastiest dinner Sam could imagine!

Things are definitely looking up, thought Sam. *Not only did I get off with light punishment, but as a bonus, I managed to lose one of those awful boots!*

10

A Slimy Surprise

That evening, as Sam and his parents sat down to eat, there was a knock at the front door. Dad pushed his chair back and opened the door. Gil and Melody stood there grinning.

In Melody's hand was a bucket, and in Gil's, a sodden black boot!

The rubber boot that looked so shiny and new this morning didn't look so shiny anymore. It was all drippy and slimy. Sam couldn't imagine putting his foot into something so gross!

"Melody and I were up the bay just now checking on my net, and guess what

she found washed up on the rocks?" Gil chuckled. "A boot and a bucket! I figured I knew who they belonged to!" he continued, winking at Sam. "Didn't find your sock though."

"Uh, thanks a lot, Gil." Sam thought that if his missing sock looked anything like the boot, it would be just fine with him if it was NEVER found!

Melody looked triumphant. This was definitely worse than being grounded!

Gil happily accepted Mom's invitation to join them for dinner. Melody slid into a chair beside Sam.

"Well, Sam, good luck for you," said Dad.

What could he mean? thought Sam. *It certainly isn't good luck that Miss-Melody-know-it-all was staying for dinner!*

Dad and Mom looked at each other and nodded.

Uh-oh, now what? worried Sam. He'd had just about enough punishment for one night.

"Now that six weeks' allowance money can go toward buying you a pair of hip waders," Mom said with a grin.

"I already have hip waders," said Melody to no one in particular.

But Sam wasn't even listening to her. Hip waders! He could hardly believe his ears!

"That is, as soon as you outgrow your lucky boots!"

They all laughed, even Melody, and Sam thought, *What a great day: a giant clam AND new hip waders.*

Life for a boy in Seldovia didn't get much better than this!

Seldovia
Sam
and the
Sea Otter Rescue

Contents

1

Hike to Sandy Cove

Sam and Neptune walked down the dirt road, past the fish cannery. Sam could hear the clinking of conveyor belts and the voices of the cannery workers. The heavy smell of fish floated on the foggy air, but Sam didn't mind. He was off to work on his fort at Sandy Cove.

Sam's driftwood fort promised to be a great place to spy on fishing boats as they chugged through the channel and out to sea. Today, Sandy Cove would be cold and wet, and most of the boats wouldn't dare to venture out in the fog where dangerous rocks would be hidden.

Sam passed the boatyard. Fishing boats sat up on wooden blocks, waiting for repairs and painting. Later in the day, the boatyard would be noisy with the whine of electric sanders and busy men with ladders and buckets of paint. This morning, it was the *whaaaooo-whaaaooo* of the foghorn on the cliff that shattered the quiet.

Just past the boatyard, he came to the spruce forest and the trail that would take him to Sandy Cove. The trees were full of birds, all singing despite the rain.

Sam loved walking through the woods on the springy moss. Today it squished like a bright green sponge. Sam stepped carefully around the white flowers of dwarf dogwood and the tiny purple violets that poked through the moss. The sound of the foghorn grew softer as the trail left the village and wound along the coast.

Sam came to a mound of old clam and mussel shells left in the woods by ancient

Indians who had feasted on them. He poked through the mound with a stick, hoping to find an arrowhead. "No arrowheads today, Neptune," he said, and continued on his way.

Next Sam passed the place where his mother came to gather wild mushrooms in the fall. He looked, but the mushrooms were still tiny spores, asleep under the moss. "No mushrooms today," said Sam.

Just ahead grew a thick stand of alder bushes. Sam stood at the edge of the alder patch and whistled and clapped his hands to scare away any black bears that might be feeding on the tender young grass. Out shot a squirrel. "Whew! No bears today," said Sam.

As they walked by a lagoon, Neptune startled a small flock of sea ducks. With a sudden flapping of wings, they took to the air. Neptune ran after them, barking. Sam chuckled, "No ducks today, Neptune."

The trail wound away from the lagoon

and grew muddy. Sam hopped from log to log, and threw his arms to either side for balance. One more log, a patch of grass, and then . . . Sandy Cove!

It was so foggy that Sam couldn't see the red-and-green buoys in the water that marked the channel for the boats. The tide was low, and Sam could hear the waves breaking on the rock ledges, but he could barely make out their shapes.

Waaa-waaa.

Sam heard, or thought he heard, crying. He listened hard, but he didn't hear it again. Maybe it was just the foghorn at faraway Lookout Point. Sometimes, noises sounded strange in the fog . . .

A Voice in the Fog

S am's fort was just as he left it, standing at the edge of the woods. Dad had helped Sam drag four big logs up the beach and arrange them in a square. Then Dad had cut long, straight alder branches and had driven them in the soft ground with a mallet. Dad had shown Sam how to nail driftwood boards to the alders, and how to brace the walls so they wouldn't fall in. The rest was up to Sam.

Every weekend since the snow had melted, Sam had come to Sandy Cove to scrounge for boards to build his walls. Now all that was left to do was the roof. Sam couldn't wait to finish his fort so he and Neptune could spend the night there.

Waaa-waaa. Waaa-waaa.

There it was again. That faint crying sound.

Sam strained to listen, but all he heard was the *whisshhh-whisshh* of the gentle waves on the ledges.

"Come on. Let's go find some boards."

Sam and Neptune set off down the beach. In a jumbled pile of tree stumps and seaweed, Sam found three large silvery boards. They would be perfect for the roof! One by one, Sam dragged the boards back to his fort. They were very heavy, and it was hard work.

Sam sat down to rest for a moment, wiping sweat from his forehead.

Waaa-waaa.

There it was again, like a sad baby. Neptune perked up her ears. She heard it too! Neptune ran down to the water and barked.

Aroof! Aroof!

Sam ran after her.

Waaa-waaa. Waaa-waaa.

It sounded as though it were coming from out on the water. Sam knew that sound traveled easily over water. Once, when he and Dad were on their fishing boat, anchored in a big bay, Sam heard voices. They sounded like they were on the boat, but when he came out on deck, Sam realized the voices were coming from a boat anchored on the opposite shore!

Waaa-waaa.

A slight breeze scattered the fog for just a moment and Sam could see the rock ledges just off the beach. Something out there seemed to move.

Sam worked his way from rock to rock, moving closer to the ledges. Although the tide was low, a good stretch of water still lay between the ledges and the shore. It was too far to jump, and Sam couldn't tell how deep the water might be.

The little shape moved again and cried. It was a baby sea otter lying right on top of the rocks! Sam could just see its fuzzy head and bright round eyes. The fog began to lift in the breeze and Sam saw that the baby was alone. Sam knew that if the fog cleared and eagles spotted the defenseless baby, they would carry it off. He had to reach it . . . and soon!

The only way was through the water. Sam waded in. It was numbing cold but only went up to his knees. So far, so good.

Step . . . step . . . step . . . Sam moved out closer to the ledges. Maybe he could make it.

Step . . . step . . . Whooosh! Sam plunged into the water up to his neck! The cold knocked the breath out of his lungs and made his head ache!

Sam struggled back to shore and crawled out. He was a good swimmer, but the water was too cold. There was nothing to do but run back to the village to get help. Sam prayed the fog wouldn't clear before he could return to the baby otter.

3

A Cold, Wet Race against Time

Sam sprinted along the trail as fast as he could in his cold, wet, heavy clothes. He didn't hop from log to log, but sloshed right through the mud. He zipped past the lagoon, with Neptune at his heels. She didn't even stop to chase the ducks.

At the alder patch, Sam didn't stop to listen for bears, but ran on without thinking. He passed the mushroom patch andthe Indian shell mound. He raced through the spongy moss. Sam was still running when he came to the dirt road.

He rounded the corner and spotted Dad's red-and-white pickup truck at the boatyard.

Dad was helping Hank Sutton paint the hull of his boat. Sam tore through the gate and skidded to a stop, gasping for breath. He and Neptune were soaking wet and covered with mud.

Between gulps of air, Sam managed to tell Dad about the baby sea otter. "He's abandoned, Dad. I heard him crying the whole time I was at Sandy Cove. The fog is lifting and I just know some old eagle is gonna see him and kill him if we don't get back there fast!

"Please, Dad. We can't let him die. You've got to come!" begged Sam.

Dad opened his mouth and looked as though he might be getting ready to say no, but Hank spoke up, "Take my motor scooter, Wally. That boy of yours doesn't look like he can run another step."

"All right, Sam," said Dad. "We'll see what we can do. Thanks, Hank. We shouldn't be long."

Dad straddled the scooter and started the engine. Sam put Neptune into the bed of the pickup truck and told her to stay. He accepted a dry jacket from Hank and climbed on behind Dad. They putted off down the road.

Just as they reached the turnoff to the trail, Sam spotted Melody Chambers, know-it-all queen of Seldovia Elementary School.

Sam was glad she was too scared of bears to walk the trail to Sandy Beach. He didn't want anyone else to know about his discovery. As they sped by her, Sam tried to look like he went for scooter rides every day in soaking-wet clothes.

The scooter bounced over the trail, past the shell mound and the mushroom place, through the alder patch and past the lagoon. In no time, they were at Sandy Cove.

Just as Sam had feared, the fog was gone and three eagles were circling in the air above the baby otter! Sam sprinted toward the rocks, waving his arms in the air.

"Get away from there! Shoo!" he shouted.

The eagles were not leaving.

Waaa-waaa. Waaa-waaa, cried the little otter.

Dad caught up with Sam at the water's edge.

"Look, Sam. I'll try to get to him, but if those eagles snatch him first, there's nothing I can do. It's just nature taking its course. You understand that, don't you, Sam?"

Sam nodded, but his eyes were fixed on the circling eagles. He didn't want nature to take its course this time.

"Hurry, Dad," he whispered, as the biggest eagle dropped lower in the sky, swooping closer and closer to the baby otter.

4

Sea Otter Rescue

Dad yanked off his leather boots, took a deep breath, and launched himself into the water with a giant belly flop. When he came up for air, he roared in surprise at the shock of the cold water.

It took Dad just a few strokes to swim across to the ledge, but it seemed like forever to Sam.

As Dad hauled himself out onto the rocks and stood up, the eagles scattered.

"Yeaaah, Dad!" cheered Sam, jumping up and down. "Way to go!"

Dad slowly approached the baby sea otter.

It was cold and tired and terrified. It didn't even try to get away. With one swift motion, Dad scooped it up and put it inside his coat. He zipped the coat up to his chin, turned and waded back into the water. Sam could hear Dad's teeth chattering as he drew near the shore.

On the beach, Dad unzipped his coat and handed the tiny bundle of fur to Sam. "You're drier than me, Sam. Put him in your jacket so he can stay warm."

Sam cuddled the baby otter. It had the softest fur he had ever felt—like velvet and very thick. It looked like a bundle of fur with two huge brown eyes peeking out. Sam put the otter next to his face. It smelled like fish, but fresh, not stinky.

Waaa-waaa. As the little baby cried, Sam saw its pink mouth with tiny, sharp teeth, like a kitten's. Carefully, he tucked the otter in his jacket, and followed Dad up the beach to the scooter. The ride back to the village went quickly. Sam could feel Dad shivering as the cool air hit his wet clothes.

Dad left Sam at the boatyard and rode home to grab some dry clothes for them. Neptune jumped out of the truck and snuffled at the unfamiliar smell coming from Sam's jacket.

"Easy, girl," he laughed.

Hank and his helpers crowded around Sam, who opened his jacket just a bit. The baby otter squirmed and cried, *Waaa-waaa.*

"You know it's not legal to keep those critters," said a man in dirty overalls. "The Fish and Game guy will have to kill it if he can't find its mother."

"Don't upset the boy," scolded Hank.

How could anyone kill a poor, defenseless baby otter? thought Sam as he petted its silky fur. *What did it ever do to anyone?*

"But, why . . . " he sputtered.

Just then Dad returned. "Come on, Sam. Let's take your baby over to the Fish and Game officer. Thanks for the scooter, Hank."

Oh no! They couldn't take the otter

there. Anywhere but there.

"Hey Dad, wait! We can't . . . "

But it was too late. Dad was already revving up the truck.

A Life-or-Death Decision

Sam climbed in and they pulled out of the boatyard.

"Dad, we can't take the otter to the Fish and Game guy. He's gonna kill him!"

"Look, Sam," Dad said quietly, putting his hand on Sam's head, "We can't keep a wild animal as a pet. You have to let nature take its course."

Sam's eyes burned as he held back tears. Nature taking its course again—he didn't like it one bit. But he could tell that Dad had his mind made up. He would just have to think of a plan. And quick. They were already pulling up to the harbor building where the Fish and Game officer worked.

As they walked into the office, a large man in a khaki shirt and khaki pants turned to greet them.

"Afternoon, Walt," he said to Dad, shaking his hand. He tried to shake Sam's hand too, but Sam kept his hands tucked into his coat.

"Well," the officer said with a grin, "What can I do for you?"

Waaa-waaa, cried the squirming shape in Sam's coat, right on cue.

"What in the world have you got there?" asked the officer. Sam tried to cover the otter's mouth, completely forgetting those tiny, sharp teeth.

"Ouch!" cried Sam as the baby otter nipped him.

"Show him, Sam," urged Dad.

Argh! Where was a plan when he needed one?

Very, very slowly, Sam unzipped his jacket. Out popped a fuzzy brown head. The

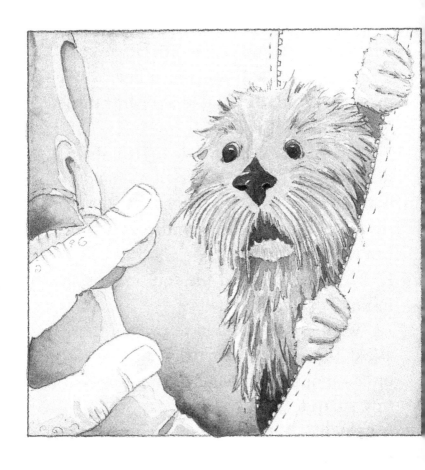

otter's bright eyes blinked and he cried even louder, *Waaa-waaa.*

"Well, I'll be darned!" exclaimed the officer. "That must be the baby that belongs to the dead female we found washed up on Stony Beach yesterday. Looked like something attacked her. Orca whale, maybe. Hard to say. We could tell she was nursing a pup, but there was no sign of him around. We figured the eagles got him."

"They almost did," burst Sam, "but my Dad swam out to the ledge and rescued him just in time!"

"Must've been a cold swim," chuckled the officer.

"It sure was," agreed Dad, "but . . . "

"You can't kill him," Sam interrupted. "He's just a baby. I won't let you do it!"

"Well, Sam," the officer said, as he cleared his throat and ran his fingers through his hair. "The problem is that he'll die anyway without his mother to feed and groom him. He's too little to fend for himself, and the law won't permit me to let you keep him as a pet."

Sam felt helpless before the Fish and Game officer, and his uniform, and his law.

The officer's big muscular arms in the khaki shirt reached out to take the baby otter from him.

"Wait!" cried Sam, stumbling backwards, "I have an idea!"

6

Sam, the Sea Otter Mom

What about a zoo?" pleaded Sam. "The one in Anchorage has a sea otter pen. I've seen it!"

The officer sighed, "Last I heard they weren't taking any more sea otters."

Sam gave him a sour look.

"But I'll tell you what," he continued, "I'll give them a call just to make sure, okay?"

Sam nodded and smiled for the first time since he'd walked into the Fish and Game building. As the officer dialed the phone, Sam squeezed his eyes shut and crossed his fingers as hard as he could.

The officer walked into another room

and talked to the zoo for an awfully long time. Sam strained to listen, but he couldn't hear a thing.

When the officer hung up the phone he looked at Sam and shook his head.

What-what-what??? thought Sam.

"It looks like you're in luck," the officer said with a grin. "It seems the zoo just shipped three young otters to a marine park in Chicago, so they have room for your baby . . ."

"Yahoo!" cried Sam, dancing around the office, hugging the otter tightly to his chest.

" . . . but hold on. They *also* said that there's a good chance your otter won't make it through the night. He hasn't been fed for at least twenty-four hours and he may be too weak to survive."

"Oh, he'll survive," said Sam with a grin. "This is one tough little otter."

"I hope so. If he's still alive in the morning, they'll send someone to pick him up. They

said I could try feeding him through the night, but he may not accept food from a bottle."

"But you've got to let me take him home," pleaded Sam. "He doesn't even know you."

Dad shook his head. "Sam, this is not a pet. You've got to understand that."

"I DO understand," replied Sam, "But he's scared. I've GOT to stay with him. I'll . . . I'll just stay here with you tonight," Sam said to the officer.

To Sam's surprise, the officer smiled. "Well, they didn't say I couldn't get a helper. I guess it won't hurt anything if you take him home tonight."

"Yeaaahhhh!" roared Sam.

Waa-aaa-aaa! wailed the hungry otter.

Dad just rolled his eyes and sighed. "What do we feed him?" Dad asked the officer.

"The zoo suggested you blend up herring, cream, and cod liver oil, and put it in a baby bottle."

Gross! thought Sam.

Dad and Sam stopped at the general store to buy the cream and a baby bottle. They went to the cannery to get the herring. And at the drugstore they bought cod liver oil. The pharmacist smiled at Sam, "This'll put hair on your chest."

"Oh, it's not for me!" Sam assured him. "It's for my otter."

They left the pharmacist scratching his head.

"Phew! What's that smell?" exclaimed Mom, when they finally got home.

"Look, Mom!" said Sam, drawing the baby otter from his jacket.

"Oh, how wonderful!" cried Mom. "Where in the world did you find him?"

While Sam told her the story, she held the baby otter and stroked his fur. He wasn't squirming anymore, and even worse, he wasn't crying either.

Dad put two herring in the blender,

then added half the cod liver oil and half the cream. *WHHRRRR!* The mix looked—well—pretty awful. And the smell! They all plugged their noses.

Dad snipped a hole in the nipple so the thick, sludgy goo could flow out. He filled the baby bottle with the mix and handed Mom the bottle.

"Here goes nothing," Mom said, putting the nipple against the otter's mouth. But he wouldn't eat.

"Looks like the otter's not hungry," said Dad. "This may not work after all."

7

A Long (and Smelly) Night

"Can I try, Mom?" asked Sam.

"Why not?" she said, handing him the quiet otter and the bottle.

"Maybe if I squeeze a little out first he'll get the idea," Sam said, squeezing the bottle until some goo came out. The baby otter licked its mouth. Sam squeezed out a little more. The otter licked again.

"He's eating!" Mom and Dad cried at the same time.

Waaa-waaa. Waaa-waaa, whined the little otter as if to say, "Quit talking and keep squeezing!"

"It looks like you've got a long night

ahead of you, Sam," said Dad. "My guess is he's going to want to eat every few minutes."

"No problem," crowed Sam, with a huge grin.

Sam made a bed for them on a blanket in front of the woodstove. He looked longingly at the couch, but Mom had been firm: no sea otters on the furniture!

Sure enough, the little otter mewed constantly, demanding to be fed. After a few hours, Sam got a big cramp in his arm. At midnight, the otter finally quieted down.

Sam curled up with the otter on his chest and they both fell sound asleep. But just as Sam was starting to dream . . .

Waaa-waaa, the otter whined right in Sam's face. Its fishy breath filled Sam's nose and mouth.

Sam forced his eyes open. "Not again!"

He stumbled to the kitchen to refill the bottle of goo. The kitchen clock said 1:20 A.M. *How can such a little otter hold all that food?* wondered Sam. *You'd think he'd have to go to the bathroom by now . . . UH-OH!*

Sam raced back into the living room. Sure enough, there was a huge puddle of— YUCK!—otter poop on the blanket!

Waaa-waaa. Waaa-waaa, cried the little otter.

Sam pushed the dirty blanket aside and fed the baby until it fell asleep again. Then he mopped up the mess with a great many paper towels. Then he put the blanket in the washing machine. Finally, he lay down and fell instantly to sleep.

Before he knew it, Sam heard the familiar *waaa-aa, waaa-aa.* He shuffled into the kitchen. Four o'clock in the morning!

Sam put the last of the goo into the bottle. He was so sleepy that he didn't notice the tiny puddle of goo on the kitchen floor. It turned out to be . . .

Incredibly . . .

Awfully . . .

SLIPPERY!

Zoom! went Sam's feet, sailing into the air.

Bamm! went his body, hitting the floor.

Slam! went the bottle, skidding across the room.

Luckily, neither Sam nor the bottle was

broken. He picked it up and fed the last of the sludge to the hungry otter. Sam was very tired. But finally, so was the otter.

This time they both snored away until daylight.

"Peeyew! What's that smell?" Mom asked, wrinkling her nose as she came down for breakfast.

"Otter poop," said Sam, with a yawn.

"Powerful stuff," laughed Mom.

"How's the baby?" asked Dad.

"I think he's going to make it," replied Sam. "He polished off two and a half bottles last night!"

Dad called the Fish and Game officer and reported Sam's success. "The zoo is sending someone to pick up the otter," reported Dad. "I'm picking her up at the airport in two hours."

Sam nodded. Despite the troublesome night, he had fallen in love with the little otter.

Mom put an arm around Sam's shoulders.

"I know it'll be tough to give him up, honey, but you have to remember that he belongs with other otters, not with us. He'll be happier at the zoo."

But Sam wasn't listening. He was wondering if the otter could live at Sandy Beach instead. Maybe he could finish his fort and stay there and take care of the otter for the summer . . .

8

Saying Good-bye

The morning flew by. Sam fed the little otter and it napped in his arms. He stroked its fuzzy head. Before he knew it, Dad was off to the airport.

Sam hoped maybe the zoo lady had missed her plane. Or maybe the plane had broken down so she couldn't fly. Or maybe an elephant caught a cold and she had to stay in Anchorage.

When he heard the pickup truck pull into the driveway and two doors slam, Sam's heart sank.

Shoot! She was here. He hadn't yet figured

out how he was going to convince her to let him keep the otter in his fort at Sandy Beach!

As they came into the house, Dad called, "Sam, come meet Miss O'Brien."

Reluctantly, Sam walked into the kitchen. "Hi," he mumbled, without looking up.

A hand reached down to shake his and he lifted his head to look into the nicest face he had ever seen. Miss O'Brien sure was pretty for a zoo lady, and she was giving him a big smile.

Sam smiled back in spite of himself.

"It's a real honor to meet you, Sam."

Me?? An HONOR? thought Sam. *Wow!*

"Not many people have been able to keep a baby sea otter alive, especially after it has been abandoned and is starving. You must have spent a long night working hard."

"You can say that again," said Sam through a mouth-stretching yawn.

Miss O'Brien laughed and continued, "I want you to know, Sam, that we'll take the very best care of your little otter. He'll have a huge pool to swim in and lots of other otters to play with.

"And," she added, "no eagles to bother him!"

That didn't sound too bad to Sam, but he still had his plan. "I don't see why he can't stay here with us," said Sam, "I could raise him in my fort at Sandy Beach and teach him everything. I could turn him loose in the bay when he gets big enough to catch his own food."

Miss O'Brien smiled her big smile again. "Oh Sam, I wish you could do just that. I know you'd be a very good caretaker. But there are just too many problems with keeping him here."

"Like what?" asked Sam, stubbornly. He wasn't going to give in, no matter how much

Miss O'Brien smiled.

"For one thing, you have a dog, don't you?"

"Yes," replied Sam, "Her name is Neptune, and she's very gentle. She wouldn't hurt anything."

"I'm sure that's true, Sam. I'll bet you've trained her well. But did you know that sea otters can catch diseases from dogs? Your otter could get so sick he could die."

"Oh," said Sam, looking at Neptune.

"Also, if you turned your little otter loose in the bay, he might get in the way of a boat, and be hurt. Unlike a wild sea otter, he wouldn't know that boats are dangerous."

Sam thought about the hundreds of boats that roared in and out of the harbor all summer. He shuddered.

"Sam, why don't you show Miss O'Brien the otter?" suggested Dad.

Sam led Miss O'Brien to the nest of

blankets. Sam had helped with mopping the floor and washing the blankets to make a new bed. The little otter was curled up on Sam's pillow.

"He's beautiful, Sam."

Miss O'Brien picked up the baby and held him next to Sam's cheek so he could say good-bye. Despite his resolve, Sam felt hot tears rolling down his cheeks. He couldn't stop them, so he turned and ran upstairs.

From his bed, Sam could hear the engine of Dad's pickup truck starting and then they were gone. So was his baby sea otter.

9

Sadness and Surprises

Sam was so sad that he couldn't eat. That night, he just picked at his dinner. On Monday, he dragged himself to school and sat by himself at lunch. He sulked all week, even refusing offers from the older boys to play kickball after school in the spring sunshine.

"Hey Sam. We need a second baseman. Come on!" urged Billy Sutton.

"No thanks," said Sam.

"Okay, you can play first base, Sam," said Darwin Chambers. He was Melody's cousin and as nice as Melody was bossy.

Normally, Sam would have jumped at the chance to play with the older boys, but today he just didn't have the heart. He also couldn't tell them why. He was afraid that if he tried to explain about his baby otter, he'd burst into tears. Then they'd never ever ask him to do anything again.

"I've got to help my Dad on the boat," said Sam. It was a lie, but it made sense. Their fathers were fishermen too.

"Maybe another day then," said Billy.

"Yeah, maybe," mumbled Sam.

By Thursday, Sam was still in a funk. Mom and Dad came into his room and sat on the bed.

"Sam, we need to go to Anchorage this weekend for supplies. Would you like to go with us?"

Sam perked up. "Yeah! Can we leave tomorrow morning?"

"I'm afraid not, son," laughed Dad, "You have school tomorrow. We'll leave on the ferry tomorrow afternoon."

Sam could hardly sit through school on Friday. This time, when he turned down after-school invitations from Billy and Darwin, it was with a happy smile.

"I'm going to Anchorage!"

"Man, you're so lucky," said Darwin. "You'll probably get to see the new movies and go to the mall and eat pizza 'til you bust."

And maybe go to the zoo, thought Sam. On the ferry, Sam hung over the rail and waved at the sea otters floating in the kelp beds. He hoped they'd have time to see his otter soon.

In the truck, Sam slept during the long drive. He hardly noticed when Dad pulled into a motel and carried him into the room.

Saturday was warm and sunny. The trees in the city showed signs of new leaves. Sam woke with the sun in his face. The motel clock said 7:10.

"Okay, let's get the errands done," he announced.

"Oh, Sam, we have a long list and then a long drive back to Homer. You'll have to relax," said Mom.

But Sam couldn't relax. He fidgeted through breakfast. He bounced up and down on the truck seat and raced up and down the aisles at the grocery store. He jumped on and off the stacks of lumber at the lumberyard, and tied knots in the big coils of rope at the marine supply store.

Finally, it was noon.

"Are we done yet?" urged Sam.

"Not yet!" said his weary parents. "We have one last errand to run before we go."

They couldn't leave Anchorage without going to the zoo! What more could they possibly need to do? thought Sam in dismay. This was the worst trip he'd ever had!

10

The Sea Otter Gets a Name

Dad turned the truck south and headed away from the city.

"Where are we going?" asked Sam.

"One last errand," replied Dad mysteriously.

Dad winked and then Sam knew—they WERE going to the zoo! Finally!

At the zoo, Sam ran through the gate, past the black bear cage and the wolverines, past the lynx and the caribou, past the sea lion tank, and skidded to a stop in front of the sea otter exhibit.

There was Miss O'Brien giving directions to a man who was mixing food in a bucket.

She gave Sam a big smile.

"Hello, Sam. We've been expecting you."

"You have?" asked Sam. He looked at his smiling parents. They had planned this all along!

"Come look at your baby," said Miss O'Brien, leading him to the far end of the sea otter pen. Sam pressed his face against the glass. He wished he could go inside but Miss O'Brien explained that adult sea otters can bite—hard—if they are scared. Thinking about how sharp the baby's teeth were when he nipped, Sam understood.

"Wow!" exclaimed Sam. It had only been one week, but the little otter had sure grown! He was practically twice as big as before. He didn't look like such a helpless baby anymore.

A big otter swam over to the baby and pulled him onto her chest.

"That female has adopted him, Sam. Her baby got sick and died about ten days ago, and now she's taken over caring for your baby. This is very unusual behavior, but we're thrilled."

Sam watched as the big otter groomed the little baby. Over and over she stroked and fluffed his fur.

"She's fluffing up his fur with air so he stays warm and dry," explained Miss O'Brien. "That's an important part of caring for a sea otter."

Sam watched the otters swim, and play, and dive, and feed. He watched them groom their fur, and roll over and over in the water. Some of them slept on their backs, their faces turned to the sun, their paws held together under their chins.

Sam especially watched the baby. He was a bit disappointed that it didn't seem to notice him.

All too soon it was time to go.

"We'll come back again this summer, Sam, so you can see how your baby has grown," said Dad, putting his arm around Sam's shoulders.

Sam nodded. He didn't feel as sad now that the baby otter had a mom to take care of it. He smiled at his own mom as she ruffled his hair.

"Sam, wait!" called Miss O'Brien. "There's one more thing I want to show you."

She led him to the front of the sea otter exhibit. On one wall of the tank were signs that told about each otter and listed the name the zoo people had given them. There was "Grumpy" and "Whiskers" and . . . hey, there was a brand new sign!

The Anchorage Zoo is pleased to welcome a new sea otter to our exhibit. The baby otter was found abandoned near Seldovia by a young boy named Sam Peterson. The 8-year-old boy nursed the starving baby otter until it could be transported to the zoo. In recognition of Sam Peterson, we have named the new otter "SAM."

Sam looked back at his baby otter. It was on its new mother's tummy, but she had paddled close to the glass. The little otter was looking right at him!

Waaa-aa, Waaa-aa, it cried.

Sam grinned at Miss O'Brien.

"So what do you think, is that a good name for your otter?" she asked him.

"It's perfect," Sam replied. "Just perfect."

Seldovia
Sam
and the
Wildfire Escape

To Marie Elyse Hoopes.
Read, Dream, Live! —S.W.S.

For Brian—who never questioned
why his muddy bike was parked
on the rug in my studio. —A.C.M.

Contents

1

Dry as Dog Biscuits

The May sun sparkling off Kachemak Bay was so bright that Sam had to squint. He was in Homer, helping out at the air service terminal where Mom worked. He did this every summer after school was out, but this year he was getting paid. *I can't wait until I earn enough to buy my X-Treme Trail Smasher!* Sam thought as he sorted a jumble of nuts, bolts, and screws into the jars that the mechanic, Stinky Swenson, had set out for him. Sam was picturing himself racing uphill on his cool new bike, with its knobby tires, fifteen gears, and front suspension.

"How's it going, Sam?" asked Stinky. "Almost done?"

Stinky's voice startled Sam out of his daydream. Sam's dog, Neptune, lifted her head, thinking it might be time to go home.

Stinky chuckled, "What you've done looks good, Sam, but you haven't done much! Think you can finish up before your mom gets back? She's due in soon."

"No problem," Sam said, sitting up straighter and nodding his head. *If I want that bike, it's more work and less daydreaming.*

Sam had just finished when he heard Mom's plane taxi up to the hangar. Neptune recognized it too and jumped up, tail wagging.

"Hi Mom!" Sam called as she dropped down from the pilot's seat. She came over for a hug, then spied Sam's greasy hands and grinned.

"Better go wash up before you get in the

plane. Are you about ready?"

"Yep, I just finished!"

Minutes later, a cleaner Sam was buckling himself into his seat in the blue-and-white Cessna. Neptune was in back. Mom checked her gauges, then taxied to the runway and pushed the power throttle forward. Gaining speed, she pulled back on the yoke.

Sam watched the ground fall away as they climbed. The radio in the small plane crackled. Through his headphones, Sam could hear Charlie Dreyer growling over the airwaves. Charlie owned the air service where Mom worked.

"November 4486, this is November 171 Delta."

Charlie was calling for Mom. Each plane had a unique number, and Mom's was N4486. Because an "N" could sound like an "M" on the radio, pilots used words instead of the alphabet letters. The word for "N" was "November." Charlie's plane was N171D, so for "D," they said "Delta."

"November 171 Delta," said Mom, "This is November 4486. Go ahead."

"Yeah, I'm inbound to Homer from Windy Bay," Charlie said. "You wouldn't believe how dry these creeks are. Dry as dog biscuits." Sam smiled. Charlie had a colorful way of talking.

"Roger that," Mom replied. "We're headed home to Seldovia and it's dry here, too. That big waterfall at the head of Jakolof Bay is just a trickle."

"Let's hope no one gets careless with a match!" answered Charlie. "What's the weather report?"

Mom told him the latest weather report at Homer showed no rain any time soon.

Sam knew this was unusual for May. In past years, as they flew over the mountains, he and his mom would see who could spot the most waterfalls created by the melting snow. But now as he looked down, the mountains were nearly bare. Below him, Sam spied Jakolof Bay and the long dirt road that linked Seldovia with the bay's boat dock. It was a favorite spot for boaters. He saw boats, clam diggers, tents, and campfires.

Sam thought hard about those fires at the edge of the dry woods. Dad had taught him the special formula for putting out a campfire: first the bucket of seawater, then the sand kicked onto the fire to bury it, and last, another bucket of seawater poured carefully over the top. Dad would repeat his formula: *"No air + no fuel = no fire!"*

It was important to put out campfires the right way. He hoped the city people camping at Jakolof Bay knew Dad's special formula.

2

A Wisp of Smoke

The next morning, Sam's dad and his crew were preparing to go herring fishing. Dad was packing canned goods and bags of pasta while his helpers carried armloads of fishing gear to the truck. Tomorrow they would leave for a month on the *Wild Rose*, headed for the fishing grounds near Kodiak Island.

Mom was paying bills, while Sam munched on cereal. The kitchen radio was tuned to the Homer station. After a moment of silence, the announcer's voice changed.

"We've just received word of a major wildfire west of Anchorage. Here's what we know so far . . ."

Sam called, "Mom, Dad! Come 'ere! There's a big fire!"

Both of his parents stopped to listen.

". . . fifty miles west of Anchorage is burning out of control due to continuing dry conditions. Firefighters and equipment from Anchorage and the Kenai Peninsula are helping combat the blaze. More later as details . . ."

Dad shook his head. "Bad news. I sure hope we don't have any fires, especially with everybody working on that one."

Mom nodded. "And with most of our Seldovia men headed out fishing, we'd really be in a pickle. What we need is some rain." She sighed, "Well, Sam, we'd better get going."

Sam jumped up. Work meant money to buy the X-Treme Trail Smasher. His old bike was okay, but it didn't have extra gears for climbing hills, or shocks for taking jumps. Dad had repaired his frame or a broken chain more than once.

He had chuckled, "Sam I'd tell you to go easy on this old bike, but I know better. Just to try to slow down a little bit, okay?"

Sam had grinned and agreed . . . sort of.

In Homer, Sam washed windows. Everything got dirty quickly from all the dust and sand blowing around. *A little rain would sure help me, too,* he thought.

At day's end, Sam and Neptune piled into Mom's plane. He fastened his seatbelt, put on his headphones, and gave Mom the thumbs-up sign. Aloft, the little plane bounced in the bumpy air. Sam loved it.

It was kind of like jumping his bike.

"Woo-hoo!" he yelled happily.

Mom pulled her headphones away and looked a little cross. "Please don't yell in my ear, Sam. It's been a long day."

Flying over Jakolof Bay, Sam noticed that the busy beach was now deserted. Then he spotted a wisp of smoke at the edge of the trees. Without thinking, he yelled into his headset.

"Mom! Look! I see smoke!"

This time, she didn't fuss about him yelling in her ear.

"Hang on. I'm going to get a better look."

Sam felt his stomach rise as Mom forced the plane to dive. She turned the yoke hard to the right and circled above the smoke in a tight turn.

"It's a fire, all right," she said. "I can't see any campers though. I'd better call it in, just to be safe. Homer base, this is November 4486."

"November 4486, this is Homer base, go ahead," Charlie answered.

"We're seeing some smoke at Jakolof Bay, just up from the dock. I've circled it and don't see any people. Can you get it checked out?"

"Roger, will do," confirmed Charlie, "I'm on it."

Mom flew over the last ridge and landed on Seldovia's airstrip. They climbed in the

Jeep and headed home.

"Hi Squirt!" Dad said at the door. He squeezed Sam's shoulder, then turned to Mom. "Charlie called. A trooper checked out your smoke. He found the campers nearby, and he warned them to watch it."

Dad dished up venison stew, then he and Mom spent the evening mending herring nets in the living room while Sam read a stunt bike magazine. That night he dreamed of jumping the X-Treme Trail Smasher through big rings of smoke.

3

A Fire Is Reborn

It was still dark when Dad sat on Sam's bed. Sam yawned and rubbed one eye.

"Why are you leaving so early? I thought we were all going down to the dock together."

"The wind came up on the bay. I want to cross open water and get behind Kodiak Island before it gets worse. I'll be fine. Just give me a hug."

After Dad left, Sam instantly fell asleep again. Several hours later, he woke to the sound of tree branches thumping against the house. Bright sunlight flooded the room. *Another windy, dry day. Dry as dog biscuits.* Sam quickly dressed and Neptune followed him to the kitchen, where Mom sipped coffee.

"'Morning, Sam! I thought I was going to have to wake you up for our date."

On Mom's day off, they always had breakfast at The Tidepool, which looked out over the harbor and was decorated with shells and crabs and pieces of coral. Today the restaurant was crowded and everyone was talking about the weather and herring fishing.

Sam was making a racetrack with his fork in what was left of his scrambled eggs, when Billy Sutton trotted in.

"Hey Sam," said Billy. "You ready to go jumping?"

Sam glanced at his mom, who was chatting with Melody Chambers's mom. Sam wasn't crazy about know-it-all Melody, but their moms were good friends, so he saw Melody more often than he liked.

"Boys, did you know Melody's cat,

Willow, had kittens?" Mrs. Chambers asked. "They're ready for new homes. How'd you like a kitten?"

Sam already knew the answer. Neptune would never forgive him. He looked outside, where she waited patiently. Neptune wagged her tail as if to say, *No kittens! Just you and me!*

"Umm . . . thanks, we'll think about it," stuttered Sam.

After promising to ride safely and be good and be home for lunch and a whole bunch of other things, the boys made their escape.

"Let's go out to my house," Billy said.

"I made some awesome ramps!"

"Cool!" agreed Sam.

With Neptune chasing, the boys rode nearly two miles out the dirt road. Sam watched Billy shift gears and climb hills easily, while he stood on his pedals and pumped his three-speed. *Not long until I have my X-Treme Trail Smasher!* he thought.

They passed dozens of new houses. Out here, the logging company had cut big stands of trees and built new roads, then sold the land. There were still lots of stumps and a few dead trees around, but families like Billy's and Melody's were happy to find land and build modern homes with hard-earned fishing money.

Billy's house looked like a mansion to Sam, with lots of different-shaped windows that reflected the sun. There was no lawn yet—just stumps and parts of trees. Billy had set plywood against some stumps to make his bike stunt course. They took turns sailing off the ramps until Sam was sore from his bike jarring each time he landed. When he borrowed Billy's bike, with its big shock absorbers, it felt like landing on a mattress. Sam was almost relieved when Billy said, "I'm hungry!"

Sam looked at his watch. It was past noon—he'd promised to be home for lunch.

"Let's go to my house," he said. "I'll race you! At least I have a chance going down the hill!"

When Sam and Billy burst through the kitchen door, they were laughing and hungry as bears. Mom was taking notes with the phone tucked under her ear. She waved her hand at them to be quiet.

"Okay," she said, "I'll get going now." She hung up and turned to the boys. "That was Charlie. Remember that campfire? The campers didn't put it out all the way, and now it's spreading. They want me to fly over and check it."

Sam had never seen his mom look so worried.

4

Worst Fears Confirmed

Mom gathered her pilot's notebook, headphones, and key, then grabbed her jacket.

"Mom, wait!" said Sam, "Billy and I can help spot the fire."

"Oh, Sam," she said, "it's too windy and rough."

Sam knew Mom would take him in an instant. He flew all the time. But would Billy get sick?

"Don't worry about me, Mrs. Peterson," Billy said. "My mom says my stomach is like a steel drum. She's a nurse, so she oughta know. I won't get sick, I promise."

Sam's mom looked hard at Billy, then picked up the phone. "Okay, but let's call your mom first."

Billy spotted the chocolate-frosted brownies on the counter and each boy grabbed a couple. They stuffed one in their mouths and the other in a napkin in their jackets.

Then Mom said, "Let's go!" and two excited boys jumped on their bikes to follow her Jeep to the airstrip.

In the plane, Sam sat in the copilot's seat. He gave Billy a pair of headphones and plugged them in. They pulled their seatbelts tight. Billy's hand slid in his jacket pocket

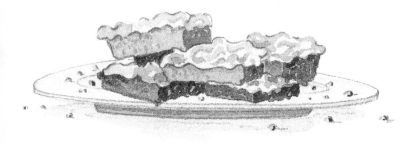

and he crammed the second brownie in his mouth.

Mom taxied to the runway and revved the engine. The engine noise was loud as they roared down the runway and, at the very end, lifted off.

After a bumpy ride, Jakolof Bay came into view, and Sam spotted it right away. The white wisp they'd seen yesterday was now a big chimney of thick gray smoke.

Mom spoke through the headphones. "I'm going to circle the smoke. Watch and tell me if you see flames. Billy, try not to stare at the ground as I'm turning. Just glance down, then look back up at the controls for a minute. Otherwise you may get sick, okay?"

"Okay, Mrs. Peterson." Billy's voice sounded small.

Mom tilted the yoke and held it as the plane made a tight circle. They bounced in the wind, and it was hard for Sam to keep his eyes on the right spot. Suddenly the wind parted the column of smoke.

"I see fire, Mom!" he exclaimed.

"Me, too," croaked Billy.

"Okay, I'm going to circle a couple more times. If you can, tell me how many trees are burning."

As Mom circled again, the plane bucked and jumped, and there was a gap in the smoke for a moment. Then the wind shifted again and the gap closed.

"Mom, I think there's five trees on fire. I know I saw two trees that were all burned up," reported Sam.

"Uhhhhh . . ." added Billy.

Mom straightened the plane and turned toward Seldovia. "Good job, boys. Let's go. It's rough!"

She pushed the transmit button and called Charlie. "Better get word to the sheriff," she said. "It's too big to handle without a crew."

"Roger, roger," replied Charlie. "The sheriff already has a call in to the Homer Ranger Station to get a crew together. It's hard—everyone's at the fire up north."

"Charlie, we'd better act fast. Too many dead trees and not enough melting snow.

If that fire gets bigger and jumps the canyon, it could burn all the way into town."

"And take all those fancy new houses with it," added Charlie, not knowing that Billy was in the plane. Sam turned to look at his friend. There was a look of horror on Billy's face.

Billy moaned, then threw up his two brownies, and his breakfast, and who knows what else all over the backseat.

5

The Battle Begins

On the ground, Sam couldn't wait to open his door. *Phew! The smell in there!* Billy climbed out looking pale and kind of shaky.

"Sorry. I've never done that before."

Mom sighed. "That's okay, but maybe next time you should go easy on the brownies."

"Yes'm," mumbled Billy. "I guess I'll go to the clinic and see my mom."

"Good idea," replied Mom, "and Billy . . . ? Don't worry about your house, okay?"

Billy smiled a wobbly smile and pedaled away. Mom pulled out the seats while Sam grabbed the hose. Soon they were clean and drying in the warm sun.

Just then, a big, yellow Cessna taxied up. "Why, that's Charlie!" exclaimed Mom.

He cut the engine and two strangers stepped out. Charlie came around to introduce them.

"Rose, this is Mitch with the Homer Ranger Station, and Preston, the chief at the Homer Fire Department. We're headed to a meeting in town—looking for volunteer firefighters. You comin'?"

"Most of our men are out fishing," Mom answered. "Can't you send a crew from Homer while the fire is still small?"

Charlie gently answered, "Rose, it's not small anymore, and it's spreading."

"Is . . . is it headed in this direction?" she asked. All three nodded solemnly.

"Then we'd better get going."

The hall was packed and noisy when they arrived. The mayor cleared his throat, welcomed everyone, and introduced the visitors. Mitch spoke first.

"The winds are pushing the fire this way. I've pulled a crew from the fire up north—but they won't get here 'til the day after tomorrow."

Preston stood. "Five men from the Homer Fire Department are coming in the morning. I just need fifteen volunteers. With my guys as leaders, that will give us five crews of four men each."

Preston looked around. So did Sam. So did everyone else. Most were older men, or city people who owned the summer cabins, and a few shop owners. They didn't look very rugged.

If only Dad and the other fishermen were here! thought Sam.

In the end, five men and three women stepped forward. That was just half of what was needed!

The sheriff called for attention. He was the size of two men, with a belly like Santa.

"I'm a big fella," he began, and several people chuckled, "but I can run a backhoe and I'm good at it. Give me some people to work the ridge. We'll cut a wide path that the fire can't cross. We'll drop trees with chainsaws, then I'll pull stumps with my machine."

There were murmurs of agreement.

"Creating a fire break is a good idea," said Mitch. "Without trees to burn, the fire goes out. But if we fight the fire at Jakolof Bay, it may not even get to that ridge."

A man stood up, "What do you mean, 'may not'! Can you give us a guarantee?"

Melody's mom called out, "What about our new houses out the road? Aren't they important?"

"What about my summer cabin?" yelled another man.

"Forget the summer cabins," cried another. "We want to protect our town!"

Sam had never seen these neighbors so upset. Then the sheriff spoke again: "Well, you fellows can go throw water around at Jakolof. I'm taking my backhoe and my crew, and we're going up the ridge to save this

town." He marched out with his followers.

It was all mixed up after that. Mrs. Chambers asked again about the new houses, but her voice was lost in the noise. The meeting ended with the mayor calling out instructions for volunteers. Sam glanced over at Melody. Tears rolled down her cheeks.

Even though she was a know-it-all, she didn't look like one right now. She looked scared, and Sam felt sorry for her.

All around him, Sam heard: "What's going to happen?" He wondered, too. His head was so full it made him dizzy to think!

6

Our Best Shot

S am!" called Mom up the stairs. "Sa-a-a-m! Time to get up!"

Sam groaned and blinked. He hadn't slept well, but Mom sounded serious and on the verge of being mad. Sam rolled out of bed and thumped downstairs.

"What's going on?" he asked sleepily.

"Sam, listen carefully," said Mom grimly. Sam realized she had her jacket on and her flying things were on the counter.

"I'm going to be in the air all day. Charlie needs extra help to bring the firefighters and their gear over from Homer. Then I'll have to fly over the fire and send reports to

the ground crews."

"Can I go with you?" asked Sam. He knew the answer would be "No," but he tried anyway.

"No, Sam," replied Mom. "I'm going to need every seat in the plane."

"But I could help you . . ." began Sam, but Mom cut him off.

"No, Sam, you have to stay here. The mayor may decide to evacuate the town if this fire gets close. I want you at the clinic so Billy's mom can keep an eye on you."

"What do you mean, 'evacuate'?" asked Sam. "Where would we go?"

"If that happens, and I mean *if*, they'll get some boats rounded up and you'll head out in the bay."

Sam was wide awake now, and he felt his stomach jump.

"But, Mom, wait," Sam pleaded. "Can't you just land and pick up Neptune and me?"

Sam's mother knelt and put her hands on

his shoulders. "If that fire makes it to the top of the ridge, it'll be too dangerous for me to land." She hugged him and kissed his forehead. "You'll be okay, Sam, and so will I. Don't worry. Just promise me you'll listen to Mrs. Sutton and do exactly as she says. So get dressed—she's coming to pick you up. And be sure to take extra warm clothes and Neptune's leash. I love you."

Sam nodded. He could feel tears filling his eyes. He rubbed them hard with his fists. Mom kissed him again and then she was out the door. Sam noticed she was carrying a shoebox—her memory box, she called it—where she kept her favorite family pictures and art stuff that Sam had made. As he dressed, he decided to put some of his favorite things in his backpack, too: a fossil of a clamshell, Neptune's puppy collar, and his worn-out, one-eyed teddy bear.

Sam waited on the sidewalk. Main Street was full of people bringing stuff to the docks.

He recognized many of them as people from new homes out on the road where Billy and Melody lived. There were lots of boxes, and a rocking chair, and a computer, and an old mirror. How would they ever fit everything on the boats? There were hardly enough boats left in the harbor for just the people. He wondered if Billy would get to bring his new bike.

Two strangers passed him, their faces and clothes black with soot. Sam guessed they might be firefighters. They didn't even notice him. ". . . fire's jumped Dark Creek Canyon," said one man. "Already burned six houses out there."

Sam shivered.

7

Where Will It Stop?

The sight of Billy and his mom pulling up in their red pickup was a huge relief. And there was Billy's bike perched on top of a pile of stuff in the back.

Mrs. Sutton rolled down her window. "Hop in, Sam. We're headed for the clinic, and you boys will need to stay there. If we have to go to the harbor, I don't want to go searching for you two."

Sam opened the tailgate for Neptune. He was about to climb into the truck when he remembered his mom's instructions. "Just a minute, Mrs. Sutton," he said. "I forgot something!"

Sam ran inside and found his jacket and an old fleece vest of Dad's. He pulled Neptune's leash off its nail, then took a quick look around the kitchen. He grabbed a picture of his parents smiling from the deck of the *Wild Rose*. He stuffed it all into his pack with his other treasures and headed out. They were already at the clinic when he realized—he'd forgotten his own bike!

The vacant lot next to the clinic was a gathering place for families from out the road. As the fire burned toward their houses, they had packed and fled into town. Sam noticed some were dabbing at tears and snuffling quietly.

He wandered among people who stood in groups near piles of their belongings. A man with a clipboard was calling out and checking off names when he heard "Here!"

"Chambers!" he called. "Anybody seen

them?" Sam looked around. No Mrs. Chambers; no Melody. Actually, he had lost track of Billy and his mom, too. But they were probably in the clinic. The man went on calling other names, but everyone else answered.

Where were Melody and her mom? Sam walked around the crowd again. They had to be here. But he didn't see them. He was looking so hard that he almost tripped over a heap of duffle bags and cardboard boxes. A cat carrier slid to the ground. The upset cat inside meowed loudly.

"Melody's kittens!" Sam murmured.

At that moment, Sam made an important decision. First he thought he'd ask Billy's mom to drive out to look for Mrs. Chambers and Melody. Then he saw their red pickup loaded with stuff—and Billy's bike on top.

The bike! Billy's fast, lots-a-gears, big shocks, hot red bike! There it was, ready to go. Sam looked at the ridge and the smoke drifting toward town. It would take too long to go home for his own bike, then slowly pedal all the way to Melody's. Without a second thought, Sam pulled Billy's bike down and set out as fast as his legs would move. Neptune ran at his side, her tongue flapping and dripping.

Sam shifted the gears so he could climb the hilly road faster. Even so, by the time he reached the Chambers's house, he was standing on the pedals and his chest was heaving. The air was smoky, and trees burned on each side of the road.

Mrs. Chambers's station wagon was loaded with bags and boxes, but Sam couldn't see anybody. Then Melody and her mom appeared out of the smoke, hands cupped to their mouths, calling "Willow! W-i-i-l-l-o-o-w!"

They spotted Sam. "Oh Sam!" cried Melody, "We can't find Willow and her kittens!"

Just then, a noise like a gunshot startled them all. They turned to see a burning tree snap and fall, almost blocking the road.

"Melody, we can't wait any more!" said Mrs. Chambers. "Let's hope Willow found someplace safe to hide her kittens."

"I won't leave her!" Melody sobbed. Sam could see she was almost hysterical. Even though he wasn't crazy about cats and he was even less crazy about Melody, his heart tightened. Right now they needed a miracle, and fast!

8

Dogs, Cats, and a Miracle

Mrs. Chambers put her arm tightly around Melody's shoulders and steered her toward the car. Melody covered her face with her hands and sobbed. Sam looked around—now where was Neptune? *What was it with dogs and cats, disappearing in the blink of an eye?!*

Sam ran around to the backyard, calling for his dog. Just as he was starting to panic, he heard barking. "Neptune! Come on!" Sam yelled.

At the corner of the big back porch, he saw his dog, head shoved under the steps, front paws digging, dirt flying through the smoky air.

"Neptunc, come on!" Sam yelled again. "This is no time to be chasing squirrels!"

Squirrels. Kittens. *Oh, my gosh!* thought Sam, *Melody's kittens!*

He raced back around to the driveway. Mrs. Chambers and Melody were waiting for him in the car. "I think Neptune found Melody's kittens," cried Sam. "Under the back porch!"

Without waiting for an answer, he ran back to Neptune. By the slam of two car doors he could tell Mrs. Chambers and Melody were coming behind him.

Sam skidded to a halt. Neptune had disappeared but there was a big pile of dirt by the porch steps. Melody and her Mom almost crashed into Sam. He opened his mouth to explain, but before he could, Neptune crawled out from under the porch with . . . a tiny mewling kitten in her mouth!

"Oh, Neptune, you're wonderful!" exclaimed Melody. She gently took the kitten from Neptune. It was wet with dog slobber and shivering, but otherwise unharmed.

Neptune dove back under the porch. Sam fell to his stomach and shimmied under, too. As his eyes adjusted to the dark, he

could see Willow and the other six kittens way back against the foundation. One by one, Neptune picked up the kittens, and Sam grabbed them and handed them out to Melody and her mom.

Only when one kitten was left did Willow pick it up herself and crawl out into the gray daylight. Mrs. Chambers swooped Willow and the last kitten into her arms before the cat had a chance to change her mind.

Coughing, eyes stinging, they sprinted for the car as spruce trees ignited with a loud *Whoosh!* Sam, Melody, and Neptune squeezed in among the bags and boxes, with Willow and her kittens.

Gravel flew as Mrs. Chambers put the car in reverse and pealed out of the driveway. Burning trees had fallen nearby but luckily none of them blocked their path. Mrs. Chambers swerved left and right, like she was driving in a video game.

As they neared town, the road widened and no trees burned along its edges.

"Phew!" exclaimed Mrs. Chambers. "That was a close call. Neptune, you are truly a hero, and Willow is a very lucky cat."

Melody wrapped her arms around Neptune and hugged her. "Neptune, you're the best dog in the whole world. I love you!"

Sam was proud of Neptune, too. This day just might turn out okay, despite the fire. It was a good thing he'd grabbed Billy's fast, fancy bike when he did.

Oh, no. Billy's bike. The fast, fancy, expensive red bike that was still at Melody Chambers's house! Sam groaned and hung his head. *Oh, no. Oh, no. Oh, no . . .*

9

State Ferry to the Rescue

Melody chattered nonstop. She was too happy and sad and relieved to notice Sam's dismay. When they reached the clinic, Sam threw open his door to escape. He mumbled, "Um, I'll tell them you're here," and hurried toward the clipboard man.

Moments later, he heard his name: "Sam! Sam! Over here!" Billy and Mrs. Sutton were waving wildly. Sam jogged over, feeling sick. He started to speak, but Mrs. Sutton shushed him. "Sam, we've been looking all over! Where have you been?"

"I was . . . I didn't . . . I . . ." Sam tried to explain, but Mrs. Sutton was talking nervously. "The mayor gave the order to evacuate, and the state car ferry heard about the fire, and they changed course to help us, and it just got here, and they're loading everybody up. We'll drive the truck on. Are you okay? Where's your dog?"

"Right here," said Sam.

"Load her in the back and let's go," she said. "Sure you're okay?" Neither one of them had noticed that Billy's bike wasn't in the truck.

The big blue ferry was full of people and cars and animals. Crewmembers ran around and urged drivers to load their vehicles quickly. Normally, boarding the ferry was a great adventure for Sam and his friends. There were so many places to explore. Today, as soon as they could, the boys went up on deck.

"This'll be cool, won't it, Sam?" grinned Billy. Sam looked at his best friend. Billy had just lost his home, but he was still so cheery. He was always in a good mood. Would Billy still be grinning when he learned his beloved bike was, at this very moment, melted into a heap of useless metal?

He groaned at the thought.

"What's wrong, Sam?" asked Billy. "You're not getting seasick, are you? We haven't even left the dock!"

Sam sighed. This wasn't going to be easy. "Billy, I have to tell you something. About your bike. It's . . . it's . . . not in the truck. It's gone."

"My bike? Where is it then?" gulped Billy.

"I used it to go find Melody and her mom. They didn't show up at the clinic, and I had to see if they were okay." In a rush, Sam told his friend about the wild bike ride, and the fire, and the search for Melody's cat, and Neptune digging under the porch. He told

Billy about the smoke, pulling the kittens to safety, and the burning trees on the road.

"Melody was screamin' her head off and Mrs. Chambers was yelling to get in the car.

I totally forgot about your bike. I'm so sorry. It's all my fault."

"I can't believe it. D-do you think maybe the fire could have burned around it?" Billy asked hopefully.

Sam shook his head. "I don't think so. It was leaning against the house, and I think . . . their house is probably gone now." Sam's voice cracked. The events of the day were catching up with him. He was worn out and scared, and missing his mom and dad.

Billy's voice cracked a little too. "That's all right, Sam. I guess you had to go help them. You're still my friend, okay?" Billy gave a shaky smile.

Sam smiled back. Just then a crew lady came over and said, "Boys, we've got cookies and hot chocolate in the galley. Why don't you come inside? It's getting blustery out here."

With her words, a gust hit the ferry. Above them, Sam saw thick, dark clouds. White spray was topping the waves in the bay, and the sun was falling behind the mountains. Looking back toward town, Sam gasped, "Billy, look!"

Billy and the crew lady stopped and turned. Sam pointed to the ridge above town. It was glowing red! Would Seldovia burn next?

10

Gifts Given and Received

That night, the winds brought heavy, low clouds that dumped a cold rain. Billy crawled out of his sleeping bag and peeked outside.

"Sam, the fire's out!" He pointed to the ridge top. It was smoking, but the awful red glow was gone. The firebreak that the sheriff had cleared, together with the wind and the rainstorm, had stopped the fire! The ferry was steaming toward town, where Mom was waiting on the docks.

After what seemed like forever, she was hugging Sam tightly. "Oh, Sam, I'm so glad to see you!" she said. Sam wanted to tell her about the fire and the wild bike ride and Melody's kittens and Neptune, the hero, but it would have to wait.

Now Mom turned to hug Mrs. Sutton. "You'll stay with us, of course, until you get resettled. Come on, I'll make some tea."

"We're gonna watch stuff here, okay, Mom?" Only one boy asked, but both mothers nodded as they left.

When Sam looked back at the water, he spied one, then four, then more fishing boats chugging into Seldovia Bay. And there was the *Wild Rose*!

"They must have heard about the fire on the radio!" Sam cried. "Let's go!"

"Yeah, let's get our bikes!" said Billy, and then he remembered. His smile faded. So did Sam's. *Could Billy really ever forgive him?*

One by one, the boat captains guided their vessels into their slips. Here came Dad! Here came Mr. Sutton! Once the boats were tied up, the engines shut down, the gear bags unloaded, and everybody hugged, they started walking home.

"Where's your bike, Billy?" asked Mr. Sutton.

"I, uh . . ." Sam stammered.

Billy interrupted. "It's a long story, Dad. We'll tell you later!" He nudged Sam and the two of them ran ahead to the house.

Sam felt even worse. If only Billy would get mad and yell or something . . . but that wasn't Billy. He would give anything to Sam or anyone else. *What could I give him that would make up for what happened?* thought Sam. Then it came to him: his savings. Sam sighed. It meant good-bye X-Treme Trail Smasher, well, until next summer. *At least I have a bike,* he told himself.

At dinner that night, the mood was light around the crowded table. The picture of Sam's parents and the *Wild Rose* was back on the wall. The grown-ups were glad that no one had been hurt. The Suttons could rebuild their home.

Billy was finishing the story of Sam and the bike and Neptune's rescue when Sam broke in: "I've been thinking, Billy. I saved all of my job money, and you can have it. It's probably not enough, but . . ."

"Are you sure, Sam?" asked Mr. Sutton.

"I'm sure," Sam replied. Billy was grinning. Dad was nodding and looking really proud. Everyone was nodding and smiling. It felt good, even if his cheeks were getting hot.

Just then there was a knock. It was Melody and Mrs. Chambers. Melody sure had a way of showing up at the wrong time!

But Melody had a surprise. "Sam, I brought you a present. Actually, it's for Neptune, for rescuing Willow's babies." She pulled a gray kitten from her coat. "I think you should name him 'Little Sparky.'"

Everyone laughed, while Sam rolled his eyes and grumbled, "Well, I think we should call him 'Big Trouble.'" At that instant, the kitten meowed loudly.

Neptune rose from her bed, gently took the kitten in her mouth, and returned to her warm place. The kitten nestled between Neptune's big paws and yawned.

"I think Neptune has a pet," Melody laughed, "and I guess 'Big Trouble' really is his name!"

Seldovia
Sam

and the

Blueberry Bear

To Caroline Emily Johnson.
Read, Dream, Live! —S.W.S.

For Brian, again. —A.C.M.

Contents

1

The Blueberry Blues

August in Seldovia was both the best month and the worst month. It was the best because salmonberries, blueberries, and high bush cranberries were ripe. It was the worst because school started at the end of it.

Sam looked around the dusty shed and sighed a big sigh. It was so big it startled Big Trouble from her nap atop a pile of fishing nets. The cat hopped onto Sam's shoulder and hitched a ride out of the shed, as Sam juggled blueberry buckets and bright orange hand rakes. Neptune spotted the berry-picking gear and danced with excitement. Sam had never seen a dog so crazy about eating blueberries!

Sam was not looking forward to school. He knew the first assignment would be to write an essay on something he did over the summer. Judges would read the essays and give cash prizes to the winners. Sam sighed again. He sure could use some money to buy the X-Treme Trail Smasher bike he wanted so badly. Last year he almost saved enough, but then he lost Billy Sutton's bike in the wildfire and gave him his savings to buy a new one.

But there was no chance Sam could win. He hadn't done anything exciting this summer. He'd fished on the *Wild Rose* with Dad. He camped in his driftwood fort at Sandy Cove. He'd flown with Mom in her Cessna delivering freight. All of that had been fun but none of it was exciting enough to win the essay contest.

Sam's know-it-all classmate, Melody Chambers, had already informed him that she had been to ballet camp (*lah-di-dah*, thought Sam) with famous dancers from New York City (*lah-di-double-dah,* thought Sam). Sam was afraid she would read her essay, throw in a few French words, and win the contest hands down.

Neptune nudged Sam's leg, reminding him it was time to go. Mom was driving Sam and Billy out the old logging road to pick blueberries. It had been a day-before-school tradition in their family for as long as Sam could remember.

Just then Billy flew into the yard on his bike, skidding to a stop and crashing into Mom's flowerpots. "Hi Sam," said Billy with a big grin. He hopped off his bike and set the pots upright. "Sorry I'm late. You got the buckets and stuff?"

"In here," said Sam, patting his backpack.

"Let's go! I can taste those blueberries now!"

They rode through town and down the

hill to the airstrip to wait for Mom to land. As they coasted to the hangar, Sam spotted her plane coming in. Then he noticed her Jeep parked nearby.

Oh no! One of the rear tires was as flat as a sand dollar!

"Billy, look!" cried Sam, pointing at the tire.

"No problem, Sam. We'll just get the spare out of the back and help your Mom change it. We'll be picking berries before you know it."

"'Fraid not. Mom's spare tire is in Homer getting fixed. We're not going anywhere."

Billy's shoulders slumped. He was always cheerful and it was almost impossible to make him sad.

Except for maybe now . . .

2

The Terrible Truck

Mom taxied her plane up to the hangar and cut the engine. She jumped out, clutching a paper sack. "Hi boys. I brought donut holes. You hungry?" she asked.

Billy's eyes lit up. He was always hungry.

Mom turned to Sam. "Did you bring the blueberry rakes, Sam?"

"Yep. But Mom . . ." Sam began.

"What?" she asked.

"Your tire is flat," he said in a small voice.

Mom looked at the rear tire. "Oh dear."

"Hey, Mrs. Peterson," Billy broke in, "Let's just borrow Mr. Peterson's truck."

"Good idea, but we can't. Sam's father

drove his truck to Jakolof Bay this morning to cut firewood." Mom shook her head. "I guess we'll just have to wait until this weekend to go berry picking."

Sam and Billy looked at each other in alarm. Miss their special day-before-school-starts berry picking?! No way!!

Both talking at once, Sam and Billy begged Mom to borrow a car to take them berry picking. The boys pushed their bikes as Mom walked beside them back into town. When they passed the Tidepool Café, Sam spotted Charlie Dreyer's rattletrap old pickup truck.

"Mom!" cried Sam, "Charlie will let us borrow his truck. I know he will!" Charlie was Mom's boss at the flying service in Homer.

"Sam, that's an awful truck," protested Mom. It was true. The once-red paint had long ago faded to a dirty pink spotted with rust. The tailpipe was attached with wire that trailed on the ground. The windshield was cracked and one of the headlights was smashed. And inside, the cab needed some serious housekeeping.

Sam and Billy dropped their bikes and burst into the Tidepool. Sam spotted Charlie at his regular table along with Danny, who ran the road grader and the snowplow.

"Hi-Charlie-Mom's-car-has-a-flat-can-we-borrow-your-truck-to-go-berry-picking-please?" Sam's words came out all in a rush.

"Hi Sam. Nice to see you too," Charlie said with a slow grin. Sam was dying to get going, but there was no rushing Charlie. "Got a flat, Rose?" he continued.

"Yes," said Mom, "and the spare's being fixed. Walt's got the truck out at Jakolof, probably half full of firewood by now."

"Firewood," said Danny, "That's what I oughta be doing today . . ."

Sam shifted on his feet. They could be here all day! "So Charlie, do you think we could borrow your truck, just for a couple of hours? This is the last day we have to pick berries before school starts."

"Sure, Sam," Charlie said slowly, "But what about bears? Danny just told us about giving some tourists a ride into town yesterday. They were out hiking and a bear chased them. Scared them half to death."

Mom turned to Danny. "Half to death," he nodded. "It was a big one."

Charlie added, "Bear stood on his hind legs and pawed the air." He stood up and waved his coffee cup and growled.

Sam could see she was about ready to cancel their trip. "But Mom, we have Neptune. She'll keep bears away," he pleaded. Mom's face softened but she still didn't look convinced.

"Not true, Sam," said Charlie. "Dogs can stir up a bear who's minding his own business."

"Okay, okay, we'll leave Neptune in the truck! Pleasemom, pleasemom, pleasemom,"

Sam chanted in desperation. Billy joined in, and the men at the table started laughing.

It worked! Mom gave in! "All right boys, we'll go but you'll have to stick close to me. No wandering off!"

"No problem, Mom. Thanks Charlie!" Sam called as he and Billy ran outside.

They opened the door of the cab and tossed in their backpacks and the bag of donut holes. They piled in with Neptune, then Mom climbed in and turned the key in the ignition. A rich gasoline smell made her wrinkle her nose. "Phew, Charlie ought to have this thing tuned!" she muttered.

She drove the truck to the dirt road that ran to the head of Seldovia Bay and the blueberry fields. As they drove, the dust from the road boiled up and poured into the cab through little rust holes in the floor.

Mom choked and sputtered, "Ugh. I can barely see. Borrowing this truck was a mistake."

"Here Mom," offered Sam, "I'll roll down a window." Together, he and Billy wrestled with the stubborn old hand crank and managed to roll the passenger window down. But instead of helping, it just made things worse. Dust poured in and filled the cab.

"Now I can't see a thing!" cried Mom, pulling over. "I'm turning around and going home!" In all that dust, Sam couldn't see her face, but he could tell by her voice that she was out of patience.

Had they gone to all this trouble just to turn around and go home again? Sam wanted to beg and plead one more time but he knew that was a bad idea with Mom so cross. He and Billy were very quiet as they wondered what would happen next.

3

Berries, Berries Everywhere

After a few moments, the air inside the cab cleared and they could see out the window. The landscape was beautiful—rolling hills thick with bushes and here and there a young spruce tree. Sam realized they were on the edge of the blueberry fields! They had made it after all!

Sam looked over at Mom, and her face broke into a big smile. "Well boys, looks like you got your wish." She got out of the truck and shut her door.

Billy let out a whoop, and he and Sam scrambled over each other to retrieve their backpacks from behind the seat. In their hurry, they knocked the bag of donut holes to the floor. Neptune dove into this unexpected treat, and the boys tumbled out of the truck and slammed the door.

They ran to where Mom stood in a swampy meadow surrounded by hills. Blueberries hung like big blue gumballs from tall bushes in the meadow. On the hillsides, the berry bushes were even bigger but the hills were thick with alder and elderberry bushes, and small spruce trees as well.

"Sam, you and Billy stay down in the meadow where I can keep an eye on you. Don't climb the hills. The brush is too dense and a bear wouldn't see you until it was almost on top of you."

"Sure, Mom," agreed Sam as he and Billy pulled out their berry rakes and buckets. Instead of handles, the buckets had long strings so you could hang them around your neck and leave both hands free to pick berries.

"Bet I can fill my bucket first," challenged Billy.

"You're on," said Sam, and they each ran to a berry-laden bush and began scooping the fat blueberries off the branches.

The late summer sun warmed the meadow, and magpies and crows flew about. The boys settled into a quiet rhythm of picking, moving from bush to bush across the meadow. Sam stopped a moment to stretch his arms. He looked up and spotted a huge bush full of berries just up the hill from where he stood. He forgot Mom's instructions and climbed up to the big bush. He noticed that beyond it were more big bushes full of berries. And beyond that, even more . . . He picked a little and climbed a little and picked a little and climbed a little.

Sam didn't realize how far he'd gone from the meadow until he stood up and looked for Mom and Billy. He could just make out their heads . . . way down below him!

Uh-oh! Better get back down the hill!

Just then, the bushes next to Sam rustled and sticks cracked. "Neptune?" he whispered. No dog appeared, but the rustling stopped. Come to think of it, he hadn't seen Neptune for quite a while. The bushes rustled again. Was it a squirrel? Sam could feel his heart beating.

Suddenly, a large black and white magpie burst from the bushes, flew up, and perched on a branch above Sam. It cocked its head and chattered at him. *Phew,* thought Sam, *false alarm.*

Then another stick cracked and the magpie took off.

Sam froze.

4

Who's in the Bushes?

The bushes rustled again. "Hello?" asked Sam in a wavery voice. No answer. The wind blew and the bushes rustled again.

Sam chuckled with relief. *It was the wind rustling the bushes,* he thought, *that's all.* Sam picked some more. There were so many berries here he just couldn't leave yet. Just one more branch and he'd head back downhill.

Sam picked and picked. His bucket was almost full. He was sure to beat Billy now. The bushes moved and Sam heard . . . chewing??! "Neptune!" he called softly. Neptune liked to pull berries from the lowest branches with her teeth and eat them.

More rustling. "Billy?" tried Sam. "Quit fooling around. You're scaring me!" Sam looked around nervously. No, he could still see Billy's red baseball cap at the bottom of the hill.

"Hello?" Sam croaked. The chewing sound was getting louder and louder and . . .

Sam peered around a small spruce tree and came face to face with a bear cub! They stared at each other for a moment, then the cub moved closer. Even though it was still a baby it was as big as Sam.

Sam waved his blueberry rake at the cub. "Stop right there," he warned. But the curious cub smelled Sam's bucket of juicy berries. It kept coming toward him. Sam took a big step backward, then turned to make his escape. There, just twenty feet behind him, was the mother bear! She stood on her hind legs. All Sam could see was a mountain of black fur.

Instantly, Sam forgot everything he'd ever learned about what to do in a bear encounter. He forgot to be quiet. He forgot to be calm. He forgot to move away slowly. Sam yelped

and threw his blueberry rake in the air. He spun around, and the bucket hanging from his neck swung out and caught on a tree branch. When Sam tried to run, he was caught by the bucket! In a panic, he yanked himself away from the tree. The string broke and the bucket fell to the ground, but Sam was free!

"Help, help!" yelled Sam as he barreled down the hill. The flying blueberry rake spooked the bear cub and it took off too, running down the hill alongside Sam! The mother bear wanted to stay near her cub so she chased Sam and the little bear down the hill as well.

Sam's legs were moving so fast he couldn't even feel his feet touch the ground. He could hear Neptune barking off in the distance. *Where is she when I need her?* Sam wondered.

5

Run Run Run!!

What the . . . ?!" yelled Billy as Sam and the two bears raced by him.

"Holy smokes!" screamed Mom as they approached.

Just then Sam tripped over a stump and fell headlong into some bushes. *That's it,* he thought, *I'm a goner.* He braced himself for a bear bite on the rear end . . . or worse!

Something jumped onto the middle of his back. "Aaahhhhiiieeee," screeched Sam, and he rolled, expecting to see black fur and giant teeth. But it was Neptune! Sam sat up quickly. The bears had run right on past him and were headed up the hill on the other side of the meadow, pursued by Neptune.

What took her so long!?! Sam thought with relief.

Billy and Mom ran to Sam. Mom was very upset. Billy looked upset too. "Geez, Sam, I thought you were a goner," he said, his eyes big and his face serious.

Mom grabbed Sam and hugged him—hard. Then came the lecture. "Sam, what were you thinking?" cried Mom. "No wait— you *weren't* thinking and you weren't listening either. What did I say about climbing the hill? What have we always taught you about encountering a bear? That's it. We're going home right now. I'm not staying out here with a boy who's not grown up enough to obey directions!"

Sam winced. "And where's your berry rake? Where's your bucket?" she asked.

Sheepishly, Sam pointed up the hill. "Uh, I guess I dropped them," he offered.

"Well, I guess they'll have to stay there. You boys head back to the truck. I need to find Neptune. She's probably chased those bears a mile away by now."

"Mom, please please let me go get my bucket. It's full of berries and I know right where it is. Besides, it's kind of on the way to the truck," Sam pleaded.

Mom looked hard at Sam. She turned and looked hard at the hill where Neptune had chased the bears. It was in the opposite direction from where the boys wanted to go, and there was no sign of bears. "Okay, Sam," she said, "But go quickly and then head right for the truck and stay there."

"Will do!" replied Sam.

"Do you really think they're gone?" Billy asked Sam quietly, when they were out of Mom's hearing.

"I sure hope so," said Sam. "That was pretty scary. The cub was cute, but then when I turned around and saw the mother right behind me . . . I thought I was gonna be a bear snack."

"When I saw you flying down into the meadow with two bears chasing you, I thought we were all done for," agreed Billy as they trudged up the hill.

"All I can say is thank goodness for Neptune," said Sam. "I wonder how she got out of the truck . . ."

Billy broke in, "Boy, these berries are huge!"

"I know," replied Sam, "I saw them and

that's why I came up here." He remembered his bet with Billy and realized any hope of winning was probably shot. His berries must have scattered everywhere when his bucket fell.

They reached the clump of bushes where Sam had been picking and found his bright orange berry rake easily, since it stood out against the green leaves. Not far away, Sam spotted his bucket lying on the ground. Amazing! Most of the berries were still inside!

Billy helped Sam scoop up the berries that had rolled out. "Your mom sure is mad," he said. "Yeah," agreed Sam, "She . . ."

Sam was interrupted by the sound of commotion down in the meadow. Mom was waving her arms and shouting.

Now what?

6

More Trouble

Mom looked up the hill and saw the boys. "Stay where you are," she called. "The bear cub came back. It was trying to get into Billy's berry bucket."

The boys stopped in their tracks. "Oh no," groaned Billy, "My berries!"

But Sam pointed out that his mom was carrying two buckets. "Looks like your berries are safe and sound."

"Sam, Billy—don't come down into the meadow," Mom instructed. "That bear cub is still around here someplace." She pointed with her arm. "Just head straight for the truck from where you are."

Sam and Billy turned and started toward the road and the truck in the direction Mom had pointed. She called out again, "Don't stop to fool around, you two. As soon as I find Neptune I'll meet you at the truck."

"Okay, Mom," called Sam. He and Billy reached the crest of the hill. They looked around at the landscape spread out below them. There, barely visible through some high alder bushes, was the dirt road, and they could just make out the faded pink of the hood of the truck. Hurray!

"I wonder where those blueberry bears are hiding?" teased Sam. He poked Billy in the back and grunted like a bear.

"Aah!" cried Billy, before he realized it was Sam making the bear noise. "Stop it. That's not funny." Sam crossed his eyes, stuck out his lower teeth, and made a bear-monster face. Billy started to giggle, nervously, then he poked Sam back and grunted his own bear grunt.

The boys descended the hill through the thick brush, grunting and poking each other and laughing. At the bottom, the bushes grew so tall and so close together they couldn't see a thing.

"I think the road is this way," said Sam.

"I think it's over that way," pointed Billy.

"We should have figured this out when we were on top of the . . ." began Sam, but he was interrupted by a sudden crashing in the bushes very close to them.

They couldn't see a thing. *Crash, crash!* It was coming right at them.

"Ohmigod, ohmigod!" yelled Billy. "Bears!"

He grabbed Sam. The thick brush exploded next to them and something black shot out.

"Bears—aahhh!" cried Sam.

But it was Neptune! Neptune, what a relief!

Sam and Billy grabbed each other and

collapsed, screaming with laughter. Neptune barked and licked their faces.

Mom heard the crashing and screaming and barking. "Sam! Billy!" she hollered. "Are you okay? Somebody answer me NOW!"

Neptune's ears perked up when she heard Mom. She turned and bounded through the bushes. Still gasping with laughter and trying to answer, the boys followed her.

"We're fine, Mom," Sam called as he pushed aside some branches. There was the road and there was the truck, and there was Mom. She looked about as upset and mad as Sam had ever seen her. Sam's smile disappeared.

"In the truck, boys. I've had enough of your silliness for one day."

For once Sam didn't protest or try to explain his way out of a situation. Quietly the boys loaded their gear into the truck and climbed in, as Neptune jumped in the back.

Mom got behind the wheel and turned the key. Nothing happened. The engine didn't growl and roar to life. No gasoline smell filled the cab. Nothing. Just a little *click-click-click* sound when she turned the key in the ignition.

Mom tried again. And again. Nothing but *click-click-click*. "I cannot believe this," she muttered.

Sam and Billy were silent. This was turning out to be more adventure than they'd bargained for. What else could go wrong?

7

Stuck in the Truck

Billy, Mom, and Sam sat in the cab of Charlie's broken-down old truck. Just as Sam was thinking nothing else could happen to make things worse, the mother bear and her cub burst out of the bushes and loped across the dirt road ahead of them. They disappeared into the brush on the other side of the road. Neptune whined. Billy let out a startled, "Aah!"

When will those bears leave us alone? thought Sam.

"You two stay put," said Mom, opening her door. "I'm going to look under the hood and see if I can figure out what's wrong."

Mom wasn't a mechanic, but from years of working on her bush plane she knew something about engines.

"Your mom's awesome," admired Billy. Billy's mom didn't even like to put gas in their car, much less look under the hood.

Mom raised the hood and poked around. After a few minutes she stuck her head in the window of the cab. "The engine won't start because the distributor cap popped off. Would you boys look in there and see if you can find something I can use to wire it back in place?"

"Sure," said Sam, and he and Billy combed through all the junk on Charlie's dashboard and the floor of the cab. There were airplane parts, leftover take-out meals, unpaid bills, notes and pencil stubs, several very dirty coffee cups, and a set of greasy coveralls. And that was just the top layer!

Sam had an idea. "Wasn't there some wire hanging off the tailpipe?" he asked. "Yeah, I think so," replied Billy. He and Sam opened the door and slid out quietly. They went around to the back of the truck and looked underneath. Sure enough, there was a length of wire that seemed like it was extra.

Sam and Billy bent the wire back and forth to break it but it wouldn't break. "Give it a yank," suggested Billy, and so Sam did.

Off came the wire, but the tailpipe thudded to the ground with it!

Mom's head shot up from underneath the hood. "What's that noise? What are you boys doing outside the truck?"

Sheepishly, Sam held up the wire with the broken tailpipe attached. "Um, we found some wire for you, Mom." He grinned.

Mom looked at the rusty tailpipe with the wire wound around it. Slowly her frown turned into a grin and her grin turned into a laugh. "This is just too much!" Sam and Billy laughed with her, and Sam brought her the tailpipe and wire.

Mom pulled and this time the wire was weakened enough so it broke off easily. She wrapped wire around the distributor cap and tried to cinch it tight. *Snap!* The distributor cap broke clean in two pieces. Now they really weren't going anywhere!

"We could walk home," suggested Billy, trying to be helpful.

"No way," Mom shot back. "It's almost four miles to town, and there's no telling where those bears have gone to."

She has a point, thought Sam. *But how will we get home?*

8

Road Grader Rescue

Mom left the hood of the truck open and they all climbed into the cab. They sat quietly, trying to figure out what to do. They were so quiet Sam could hear Billy's stomach growling. So could Mom.

"Where's that sack of donut holes?" she asked.

"I think Neptune got them," said Sam. They looked in the back. Neptune was fast asleep in the sun, full of donut holes and bear-chasing adventure.

"Is that an engine I hear?" wondered Billy.

"No, it's just your stomach growling!"

teased Sam. He and Billy poked and pushed each other.

"Wait a minute, boys—stop. I think Billy's right," said Mom.

They listened. Sure enough, it was an airplane engine, and it was coming closer. Charlie's yellow plane came into view overhead. From somewhere in the mess on the floor of the cab a radio crackled. Sam could hear Charlie's muffled voice.

"Find that radio!" cried Mom, and the boys pawed through the debris.

"Got it!" called Billy, pulling a portable radio out of the pocket of Charlie's work coveralls. He handed it to Mom.

"Charlie, Charlie, this is Rose. Do you read me?" she spoke into the radio.

"I copy you, Rose. I'm en route to Windy Bay. Good thing I spotted you—looks like you've had a breakdown." Charlie had seen the truck with the raised hood from the air and knew something was wrong. "You waiting for bears to come fix the truck?"

"Charlie, this truck is a nightmare!" scolded Mom. "The distributor cap came off and broke in two, and now the tailpipe is off also."

The radio chuckled. "Guess it might be time for a new truck," said Charlie. "I think Danny is driving the road grader somewhere around here. I'll try to raise him on the radio and get him to pick you up."

"Thanks Char ..." began Mom, but she was interrupted by another voice on the radio.

"Hey Charlie, I copied your radio call," he said. "I was headed to town but as soon as I turn this thing around I'll go out and pick them up."

"Roger that. Thanks, Danny. November 1-7-1 Delta clear," crackled Charlie as he signed off.

"Thanks, Danny. I'm clear," echoed Mom as she signed off too.

It was just a few minutes before Danny

and the road grader roared up the road toward them. Danny ground to a halt and opened the door of the cab high above them.

They climbed up the ladder into the cab. The cab was small—maybe the size of a telephone booth—and Mom and Sam and Billy were wedged in tightly behind Danny. Neptune managed to scramble up and squeeze in by Mom's feet.

Danny grinned. "I don't normally pick up hitchhikers, but I hear there are some hungry bears in the area," he said with a wink.

"Very funny," said Mom, trying not to smile.

Twenty minutes later they were back in Seldovia, dusty and rattled but safe. They thanked Danny for the ride, walked Billy to the clinic where his mom worked, and then headed home.

Sam was exhausted. Dad had cooked steaks on the grill—Sam's favorite dinner. Normally he would have devoured his steak

and talked nonstop to Dad all about his adventures. But tonight, Sam was almost too tired to eat.

When he finally dropped into bed, Sam sighed. The soft blanket, the cool pillow— he could feel himself drifting . . . off. . . . If only . . . the first . . . day . . . of school . . . wasn't tomorrow . . . and oh-my-gosh-the-essay-contest! Sam's eyes flew open and he began to worry. Then, he realized the day had given him a great topic. He smiled sleepily, closed his eyes again, and fell . . . into . . . a deep . . . blueberry . . . sleep . . .

9

Essay Day

In the morning, Sam awoke with a feeling of dread. Summer was over! No more freedom, no more fun! Aaagh! Even the bowl of blueberries with cream he had for breakfast wasn't enough to make up for his first-day-of-school blues!

Sam trudged to school. On the playground, Sam could see Melody acting like a princess, turning pirouettes and showing off her ballet moves. Then Sam spotted Billy. "Hey," said Sam.

"Hey yourself," replied Billy. "How are you feeling after our big adventure yesterday?"

"Tired," Sam answered. "And worried

about the essay contest. What're you going to write about?"

"Can't tell you." Billy said with a grin, "It's a surprise." Sam got a funny feeling in his stomach. What if Billy wrote about the blueberry bears too? Billy was a much better writer than Sam. If Billy chose the same topic, Sam didn't have a prayer of winning that cash prize!

"How about you?" asked Billy.

"Umm, I don't know," Sam mumbled.

Sam was relieved to hear the bell ring. He and Billy and all the other students raced to their classrooms. Everyone had until the end of the day to write their essay: "What I Did This Summer." At the end of the day, they would hand in their essays to the teacher.

Then a group of community leaders gathered to read the essays and pick the eight best writers. Those eight students got to read their essays at a special assembly on Saturday night. It was a big deal and most of the town filled the bleachers in the school gym to listen and find out who would win the grand prize.

All day, Sam wrote and wrote. He did a lot of erasing too. He broke his pencil twice and had to resharpen it. He told the story of the blueberry bears like he was writing a letter to his grandmother. He tried to remember all the details and make his story as exciting as the day had been. Sam handed in his finished essay just as the 3 o'clock bell rang.

Billy caught up with Sam outside. "Hey Sam, want to go fish for salmon off the bridge? Darwin has some new lures we can use." Darwin Chambers, Melody's cousin, was as nice as Melody was bossy.

"Sounds good," agreed Sam, but he was still worried. "Hey Billy, what did you write about anyway?" he added.

"I told you already, Sam. It's a big hairy surprise!" Billy shouted as he took off on his

bike. "C'mon! We've got fish to catch!"

Sam peddled after Billy. *A HAIRY surprise?* he wondered. *Billy must have written about the bears, for sure!*

Sam was unusually quiet for the rest of the afternoon. They fished and each of the boys caught a salmon. Sam rode his bike home with one hand, holding the big fish by its gills in the other. With no gears and just one hand, it was hard to ride up the last little hill to his house. He wished more than anything he could win the contest prize money and buy a new bike. But how could he win if Billy wrote about the bears too?

During the next few days, Sam saw some of the essay contest judges around Seldovia: Mrs. Dodge, the white-haired librarian, the town doctor, Dr. Stott, Mr. Farnham, the mayor, and Mr. Fenwick, a retired schoolteacher. They all smiled at Sam. Did their smiles mean something? Or were they just being friendly? By Friday, Sam was glad the week was over.

That night before bed, Sam pulled out his old stuffed black bear from the back of his closet. He was too old for sleeping with toys, but something made him want to prop the saggy old bear on his pillow.

"Wish me luck!" he whispered.

10

The Contest Surprise

On Saturday morning, Sam raced his bike to the post office. That's where the winners were posted. If it was going to be bad news, Sam wanted to be sure he saw it before anyone else.

But it was too late. As Sam pedaled into the parking lot, Danny drove by in the road grader and called out, "Congratulations, Sam."

Congratulations? thought Sam as he jumped off his bike.

There was the notice. And there was his name! "Sam Peterson—Encounter with Blueberry Bears." He scanned the list. There was Melody Chambers, no surprise. Mary

Rutledge, Ian Hatcher, a few more names, and . . . "Billy Sutton—Ancient Treasures at Fossil Point."

Fossil Point! Ancient Treasures! No bears? Hey, maybe he had a chance to win after all! Or did he? Fossils and ancient treasures sounded pretty interesting.

By the time Sam got home again, Mom and Dad already knew he was a finalist. News traveled quickly in Seldovia.

"Good job, Sam," Dad said. "We can't wait to hear your essay tonight."

Then it hit Sam—he'd have to get up in front of the whole town and read. Yikes!

By dinnertime, Sam was so nervous he could hardly eat. He pushed food around his plate, and then put on the clean shirt Mom handed him. They arrived at the school gym for the assembly to find it was already crowded.

Sam's teacher steered him up on stage to sit with the other finalists. Sam slid into a seat next to Billy. To his dismay, Melody sat down on his other side. She was wearing a ballet tutu and some funny shoes!

"I'm going to read in costume," Melody announced. "It will help bring my words to life!"

Sam rolled his eyes. "How about you, Sam," Melody teased, "where's your bear costume?" Sam scowled but was saved from having to respond when the school principal announced the start of the program.

Mary Rutledge was first, reading about helping her dad hang wallpaper. It was a very funny essay—Mary wrote about how she stepped in the bucket of wallpaper paste and went flying over backwards, bringing the wet wallpaper down on top of her. The audience laughed a lot.

Melody was next. Her essay was full of big French words, which she pronounced flawlessly. She demonstrated some of the ballet moves, even standing on the tips of those funny shoes. Secretly Sam was impressed. So was the audience, which clapped loudly.

Three more readers, and then Sam. He stood up and began to read. After a couple of sentences, he forgot all about the crowd. He read like he wrote, as though Grandma was right there and he was telling her about his adventure. He was dimly aware that the audience oohed and aahed and laughed at all the right places. When he was finished the audience cheered. Sam sat down. *Not too shabby,* he thought.

Another girl read, but Sam didn't even hear her. He was too busy daydreaming about the new X-Treme Trail Smasher he was sure would be his.

Billy read last. His essay was about a trip across the bay to Fossil Point with his dad. They collected huge rocks full of fish and clam fossils to decorate the chimney of the fireplace they were building in their new

house. Their old house had burned in the forest fire and as Billy read, Sam could see people in the audience wiping away tears.

Billy finished with an inspiring message about not letting a tragedy—like losing your house in a fire—get you down. Instead you should look ahead and rebuild your life. Not only did the audience applaud, several people jumped to their feet and cheered.

Sam's heart sank. He was foolish to think he ever had a chance to win the grand prize!

The principal said a few more words about how proud he was of the finalists. *Okay, okay,* thought Sam, *just get to the winners!*

But no, the principal went on and on. He thanked the judges. He thanked the teachers. He thanked the parents. Sam thought he would explode he was so impatient!

Finally it was time. One of the judges handed the principal a card. "Third place goes to Mary Rutledge," he announced. Mary accepted her twenty-five-dollar prize with a grin.

"And second place . . ." began the principal. Sam closed his eyes, expecting to hear his name. He thought to himself that the fifty-dollar prize for second place was better than nothing. ". . . goes to Billy Sutton," the principal finished.

Sam's eyes flew open. *Billy? Does that mean I didn't win anything?* he wondered. His head was spinning. *Maybe my essay was no good after all . . .*

But then Sam heard the words, "And the two-hundred-dollar first prize goes to . . . Sam Peterson!" He had won!

Sam was in a daze as he walked to the podium and shook the principal's hand. "Congratulations, Sam," said the principal and he handed Sam an envelope.

The envelope! Inside it was two hundred dollars! With that money, plus his savings, Sam could finally buy the X-Treme Trail

Smasher bike! The audience applauded, and Sam looked out, grinned a giant grin, and bowed deeply. The audience laughed and cheered.

In the crush of people leaving the gym, Sam found Mom and Dad. They hugged him and congratulated him.

"We made a big blueberry pie to celebrate," said Dad.

"And we invited Billy and his folks over for dessert," added Mom. "Let's go."

Sam didn't need to be convinced. He was starving. The Suttons were already at the house when Sam and his parents arrived. After lots of handshaking and backslapping, they sat down to the best blueberry pie Sam had ever tasted: tangy blueberries, a flaky cinnamon-sugar crust, and vanilla ice cream melting alongside.

Sam and Billy talked about what they would buy at the bike shop in Homer. Billy wanted a fancy bike pump so he could fill his tires without going to the gas station. Sam wondered what color X-Treme Trail Smasher he would get.

Just then, Neptune wandered in with something in her mouth. It was black and fuzzy and covered with drool.

"Eeewww," cried Billy. "What's that?"

Sam looked closely, then laughed. "It's my old bear. Last night I pulled it out of the closet for good luck. Now I guess it belongs to you,

Neptune. I seem to have all the good luck I need!"

Neptune wagged her tail and trotted over to the woodstove. She lay down with the soggy old bear between her paws. Sam and Billy helped themselves to another piece of pie and joined Neptune in front of the fire. They spent the rest of the evening planning all the places they would explore on their X-Treme Trail Smashers—places far away from any blueberry bears!

CPSIA information can be obtained
at www.ICGtesting.com
Printed in the USA
BVHW01s0657120318
510116BV00003BA/19/P